T0278204

Hospital

Sanya Rushdi

HOSPITAL

Translated by Arunava Sinha

LONDON CALCUTTA NEW YORK

Seagull Books, 2023

First published in Bengali as *Haspiṭāl* / হসপিটাল by Bahiḥprakāśa

ISBN 978 1 80309 172 3

British Library Cataloguing-in-Publication Data
A catalogue record for this book is available from the British Library

Typeset by Seagull Books, Calcutta, India
Printed and bound by WordsWorth India, New Delhi, India

Hospital

1

My morning starts with Luna Apa's email. She has sent me four of Claude Monet's paintings. She wants me to write down my thoughts about any of them, or draw a picture inspired by them. She thinks it's harmful for me to spend too much time on Facebook or on the computer, and so this alternative to pass the time.

How do I explain to anyone that I don't like drawing pictures, and I'm not very good at it, either? Still, I have to do it, she's asked me so many times.

So I sit down with Monet's *Bridge Over a Pond of Water Lilies*. At first I decide to sketch what Monet had painted, but then I see my drawing move in a different direction—a pond, within it a small island connected to the mainland by a footbridge. What's more, the bridge looks a bit like a train, and its last step leads to a lotus.

There's just the one lotus in the pond, which, because of its long stalk, sometimes wanders off towards the casuarina trees to the left of the bridge, sometimes towards the willow trees to its right, and sometimes close to the bridge itself. Half of a large tree on the mainland can be seen in the distance. The plants around it are flowering, the birds are flying near the clouds. Flowers are blossoming between the two clusters of trees on the island too.

I upload the completed drawing on Facebook. At once Amma calls out from the ground floor, 'Luna, Sunny, are you up? Come down for breakfast girls, it's so late already.'

'Coming, Amma,' Luna Apa and I answer in chorus.

Luna Apa says funny things and makes me laugh as we go downstairs. Laughing makes me feel fresh, as though nothing happened last night.

At the breakfast table, Luna Apa says, 'Santu, see, here's some brown bread and some brown Nutella, and there, that box of books is brown. And look, Amma is stirring the pot with a brown spatula.' She smiles. So do I. I feel a bit embarrassed too.

Why did all those things happen to me last night? I'm not frightened easily, why this sudden fear of brown?

Everything was fine. I had switched off the light and gone to bed when I suddenly felt surrounded by brown objects—brown leaves, the brown floor, a brown carpet, brown coffins.

I ran to Luna Apa's room and knocked on her door. 'What is it Gubloo, are you scared?' she asked, holding the door open.

'Hmm,' I said. 'Can you think of something nice that's brown? I can only think of dead things.'

'Oh yes, so many nice things. Fresh bread, cake, chocolate, pianos, bookshelves, and so much more.'

Me (somewhat relieved): That's true, you're right.

Luna: Go to sleep. I'm up, so just knock on my door if you feel uneasy or need anything. Do you want to sleep with me?

Me: No, I'm good.

'Oi Santu, where are you lost now? Have you fallen asleep?' Luna Apa asks.

'No, I'm not asleep,' I reply, looking at her.

'Finish your breakfast, Maama and the rest of them will be here any moment.'

'Oh really?'

'Yes, Amma just said, don't you listen to anything?'

'Hee hee, not this time. Which of them is coming?'

'Both.'

'OK.'

The bell rings as soon as I finish breakfast. Both our maamas and maamis are here, along with my cousins. Usually, I'm the one who plays host at home, but this time the girls don't let me do anything, they take care of everything themselves.

Farid Maama says something about someone's picture (does he mean photograph?) turning out superbly, accurately representing a social system. One of my cousins strongly opposes him and says it's a complete failure, absolute rubbish. A house, its door almost as big as the house, a massive lock on the door and the lock itself is the key—what on earth is this? Is it even possible?

Somehow, I feel they are commenting on the picture I drew earlier this morning.

I don't want to hang out with them any more. I go to my room and start thinking about why I was frightened last night. Was it a momentary fear, or had it been growing slowly since that lunch we went for? The house where we'd been invited had an enormous wooden deck. Someone saw Luna Apa and me sitting on a bench at one end of the deck and said, 'There's a furnace burning just below that bench, the deck might collapse.'

I felt kind of frightened at this.

It was true, the deck didn't seem too strong. Luna Apa laughed it off, though. I went inside, where the women were sitting. Several seats were unoccupied. I was about to sit next to one of the women when she picked her bag up from the floor and put it on the empty chair. The same thing happened with all the other free seats.

Why did all of them behave that way?

As I think about this, I hear the guests downstairs preparing to leave. I go out to say bye to them from upstairs.

Returning to my room, I Facebook for some time and listen to music. But I cannot do either very long. These days my eyes close with sleep whenever I switch on the computer, but then when I try to sleep I feel a cold pressure inside my head. Like my head's about to split open. Sometimes my skin seems to burn.

When I go downstairs and tell everyone about this, Abba says, 'I think you need to see the doctor, baba.'

Me: Hmm.

Amma: Yes, it's been a while, ma.

Luna Apa: Or I can ask CATT to come home too. They have doctors and others to assess the situation.

Me: OK. Will they assess the conditions at home too?

Luna Apa: Yes.

Me: Then that's best, probably.

Luna Apa: All right, I'll ask them to come tomorrow.

Me: OK.

2

People from CATT keep visiting me at home every day over the next two weeks. Mostly two at a time, often with a doctor in tow.

I am forced to go back on medication. It isn't clear to me why they are forcing medicines on me without assessing my living conditions first. Maintenance? But for that I have my psychiatrist.

Why has the CATT team raised the dosage of my medicines? Why for that matter do they interrogate me every day, why don't they talk to any of the others at home? Do they think my psychosis is back?

What I can do for now is be patient and answer all their questions, so that they realize I'm OK. So that's what I'm doing, responding calmly to everything the two young men from CATT keep asking.

Man 1: Hi, my name's Nick. Your name is Sanya, am I right? Am I pronouncing it correctly?

Me (with a smile): Yes, you've got the pronunciation right, I'm Sanya.

Man 2: And I'm Gagaan.

Me (smiling): Hi Gagaan.

Gagaan: Do you know why we're here?

Me: My sister asked you here.

Gagaan: Why has she asked us?

Me: Because I feel a sort of pressure in my head, and sometimes my body feels like it's on fire.

Nick: Will you tell us what kind of pressure? Sharp or blunt?

Me: Blunt. Cold and blunt.

Nick: Are you taking anything for it?

Me; No, can I?

Nick: Yes, you can. We'll give you some medicine.

Me: OK.

Nick: Your family seems worried about you. Any idea why?

Me: They're the best people to answer that.

Gagaan: Do you think there's anything to worry about?

Me: No.

Nick: They were saying you don't spend time with them, you're alone in your room all the time.

Me: Nothing new there, I've always been like that. It was only during my depression that I just couldn't be alone, I needed company to survive, I needed conversations. And the fact that I did all the housework when my mother was ill was because my family needed me to do it at that time. This doesn't mean that Sanya is who I am.

Nick: So you've fully recovered now?

Me: That's what *I* think.

Nick: Have you ever had a serious illness that needed you to stay in hospital?

Me: Yes, I had psychosis in 2009 and 2010.

Nick: Will you tell us a little about that experience?

Me: I used to feel so very unsettled, there was this bad feeling that stayed with me all the time. As though someone was trying to get me to do something by force, because if I didn't there would be some serious harm. I was so troubled I couldn't sleep. I used to think someone was influencing the people around me, preventing them from being their true selves. Something like that.

Gagaan: Did you see codes everywhere, in newspapers and on the TV and the internet?

Me: Yeah, I did. My father had a dustbin, I'd even see codes in the papers and receipts he threw into it.

Nick: You don't see them now?

Me: Ha ha, no. I only saw them during my illness.

Nick: Do you know your sister's also quite worried about you?

Me: Yeah, she always worries a bit too much.

Nick: Luna was saying you've seen some things on Facebook too?

Me: Would you say those are codes? All those symbols that artists and poets use to express themselves?

Nick: What happened exactly?

Me: Luna's already told you.

Nick: We'd still like to hear it from you.

Me: The thing is, I have a friend on Facebook who's a writer and an artist. A common friend of mine and my sister's. Most of my friends are on Facebook, that's why I spend so much time there, which some people don't like. Anyway, this friend of mine, this artist and writer, posted some of his work on Facebook. I felt that there was a continuity in the way he posted some of his artwork and writing one after another. I felt he was probably connecting with and responding to some of my posts.

One of his later paintings suggested he was proposing to me. I took two days to think it over. When I felt I was willing, I hit a like on his painting. And once I did, he started using Facebook again. Those two days that I stayed away from Facebook, so did he. Of course, this is just my impression, it could be right or wrong, I don't know. I told Luna about this and she said no one communicates this way, she said I was wrong to think the way I was thinking.

Nick: What do *you* think?

Me: I don't know.

Gagaan: Tell us, did you ever get married?

Me: Yes, I did. It ended after my second psychotic episode.

Nick: I'm very sorry to hear that.

Me: Nothing to be sorry about. I'm happy that he's well.

Gagaan: Your father said you'd been to Sydney. For your PhD.

Me: Yes, but I left it incomplete. I came back to Melbourne with a Master's degree. Sydney was where I met my ex.

Gagaan: OK. And then you came to Melbourne and got married?

Me: Yes.

Gagaan: How long were you married?

Me: Eight years.

Gagaan: I see. And what was your Master's topic?

Me: The effects of mercury and cadmium on microtubules.

Gagaan: I see, both are heavy metals, harmful for the body.

Me: Yes.

Gagaan: How do you pass your time now? What do you do all day?

Me: I listen to music, do some Facebooking, try to read a bit.

Gagaan: Read what?

Me: Psychology. What I used to study before I fell ill in 2009.

Gagaan: Was it the stress of studying that made you fall ill?

Me: I don't think so, I love studying, it doesn't stress me out.

Gagaan: OK. But don't let it put pressure on you, even things you love can be stressful if you overdo them.

Me: All right.

Nick: And switch the TV or computer off an hour before you go to bed. Often the glow doesn't let us sleep.

Me: All right.

Nick: Ok, that's all for today. We'll be back tomorrow. Let me give you your medicines before we go. (Hands them over). This one, you've been taking for the past few days, why don't you take it while we're still here. The sleeping pill is only if you need it.

Me: But this is an anti-psychotic pill.

Nick: Yes, it cures a lot of things, including the conditions you mentioned. It's only short term, you won't need to continue with it.

I get a glass of water and swallow the tablet.

Gagaan: All right, we'll go now. See you again tomorrow. Bye.

Nick: See you tomorrow.

Me: See you.

After they leave, I take the washed clothes out of the washing machine and into the backyard to hang them out to dry. This Nick guy is so articulate, he made me very comfortable. I really liked talking to them. I talk to myself as I hang the clothes on the clotheslines. Can people hear me think? Let them.

Once I've put all the clothes out to dry, I see a storm building up. I stand near the camellia tree. Small dry leaves flow in from who knows where, and shower me like rain. Oh, what a feeling!

3

A sudden jerk wakes me up. Where did it come from? I check the time on the iPad. It's exactly 3 a.m. My eyes have got used to catching the time at such precise moments. I no longer ask why it happens to me. How will I find the answer even if I ask? Where can I find some relief? In the holy Quran, perhaps? The very old Quran I used to have in my room is now on a shelf in the lounge downstairs. If I clatter down the wooden stairs at this hour of the night, Abba and Amma are bound to think something's wrong with me.

So I take off my slippers and go down the stairs, barefoot. I peep into Abba and Amma's room—no, I haven't woken them up. I go towards the lounge where my favourite Quran, the one I'm most used to, lies on the shelf along with several others. I pick it up and tiptoe back upstairs.

I flip through the holy Quran. I'm not looking for anything in particular, I'm only trying to find something that will give me some peace of mind. Turning over a few pages, I ask myself whether the Bengali translation of the Arabic verses is accurate. Running a search for Surah Al-Jinn on the internet, I discover that it's not only the translation but also one or two words in the surah written in Arabic script that don't match the ones in my copy of the Quran. I rise to my feet to get Abba's copy from his study. I want to check which one is right. When I reach the stairs, I see Abba standing at the bottom.

Abba: Not asleep yet, baba? Can't sleep?

Me: I just woke up.

Abba: Why are you awake so late at night, ma, are you scared?

Me: No, I'm not scared.

Abba: Wait, I'm coming upstairs.

Me: No need, I'm not scared.

Abba: Why are you standing there then, baba, do you need something?

Me: I was on my way to get your copy of the Quran from your study.

Abba: Shall I get it? Shall I read the Quran to you?

Me: No, no need. I just wanted to check something in it.

Abba: All right, let me get it for you.

Abba comes up the stairs quite quickly with the thick Quran. We go into my room. I remove the clothes stuffed onto one of the chairs so that Abba can sit, while I take my usual chair with the broken armrest.

Me: Why did you take the trouble to come upstairs, baba? I only wanted to check something, it wouldn't have taken more than five minutes.

Abba: It's no trouble, ma. I'll get the chance to brush up on the Quran myself.

Me: But at this hour of the night?

Abba: We're both awake anyway.

Me: All right then, read to me.

Abba puts the Quran on my desk and begins looking for something in it—near the beginning, around the end, in the middle. As he searches, his eyes keep drifting towards the darkness outside my open window.

Is Abba trying to contact someone? Why are all these helicopters passing by so noisily at this hour of the night? Is my window visible from the helicopters? Are they photographing me? But why? Who are they?

I shrink into myself and my skin begins to prickle. At that moment Abba announces that he has found Surah Yasin. 'Why don't you go to bed, dear?' he says. 'I'll sit near you and read the surah, you can go to sleep if you're sleepy, I'll switch the lights off before I go.'

For some reason I find no comfort in such a considerate proposal. On the contrary, I feel angry. 'No, I'm good in my chair,' I say.

Abba starts reading the surah. I had no idea Surah Yasin was so long. I start dozing off towards the end. Finishing quickly, Abba says, 'Go to bed, baba, I'll go now.' I fall asleep almost as soon as my head hits the pillow.

I wake up to someone hammering on my door. Almost simultaneously, the door pushes open and a face comes into view. Annoyed, I ask, 'Why have you come upstairs, Amma? Have you forgotten the pain in your foot?' She says, 'I've been trying to wake you up for a long time, baba. Then I thought, maybe you didn't sleep all night, that's why you're still asleep.'

Me: What do you mean, still asleep? What time is it?

Amma: Eleven. The CATT people are here. You have to come downstairs, ma.

Me: All right, I'll be there in a minute.

I wash my face quickly, wrap my scarf properly around myself and go downstairs. I find the entire family seated in the lounge. The small room is filled with people now. Nick is seated at one end of the three-seater, and Luna Apa at the other, leaving the middle seat free. Abba is in the high office chair next to the three-seater, on Nick's left. Amma is in the single-seater opposite Nick. The single-seater near the entrance to the lounge and the tub chair next to it are both available. I take the single-seater.

Nick: Good morning, did I wake you?

Me: No, I should have been up by now.

Nick: Did you get enough sleep?

Me: Yes, I did.

Nick: Excellent. Sleep is essential.

Me: Hmm. Gagaan didn't come?

Nick: No, he had to go somewhere else. I'll let him know you asked about him.

Me: No, I didn't exactly ask about him. He said yesterday you'd be here again today, so I thought both of you would come, that's why I asked. Anyway, would you like some tea or coffee?

Nick: Thanks for offering, but I've had my breakfast already. I don't want anything now. You go ahead and have some if you like.

Me: I'll have some later.

Nick: OK. What did you do after we left yesterday?

Me: Nothing much. Went to the bank, did some housework, listened to music. That's all.

Nick: Did you go to the bank alone?

Me: No, my mother and sister went along with me.

Nick: I see. Something important?

Me: Yes, important from the viewpoint of my faith. I went to stop receiving interest from the bank. The Quran says it's wrong to accept interest. Although I'm not sure if this applies only to banks or to other things too.

Nick: I don't think it's about banks, there were no banks at that time.

Me: Oh yeah, that's right.

Nick: You didn't study psychology yesterday?

Me: I wanted to, I tried, but I don't think it's possible at home.

Nick: Why not?

Me: I can't concentrate at home. I feel a pressure in my head all the time, my eyes close as soon as I sit down at the computer.

Nick: Really? Why do you think this is happening?

Me: Personally, I feel technology has developed so much it's difficult to keep pace with it.

Nick: Of course. It's not you alone, many of us feel that way. But why do you say this now?

Me: Because I think the cameras on laptops and most computers nowadays are for monitoring and controlling us.

Nick: I see. Do you think you'd be able to concentrate on your studies if you stayed somewhere else for some time?

Me: Yeah.

I notice Nick is sitting with his legs spread out, he is wearing baggy shorts. Every time I try to look at him, my obscene gaze keeps drifting into his shorts. My face darkens in shame at my repeatedly straying eyes. I feel particularly bad because I'm trying to become a faithful Muslim who wears a veil. Lower your eyes, Sanya, I keep telling myself. I lower my gaze.

Nick says, 'We have a few community houses available to us. Here's a brochure, you can check it out.'

I feel Nick said 'you can check it out' with some emphasis. My reserve is dispelled a little. I examine the brochure. Neat buildings.

'Do they charge rent?' I asked.

'No, there's no rent. But you may have to contribute for groceries. If you like the arrangement, this shared accommodation, I can send someone from my team tomorrow morning to take you there.'

'Oh no, there's no need to send anyone,' says Luna Apa. 'Give us the address, we can drop her.'

'Actually, that's not how it works,' Nick says. 'There are some formalities that need one of our team members.'

'But that can be done even if we drive Sanya there,' says Abba.

Amma and Luna nod.

'We can follow your car, but let Sanya go in ours,' says Amma.

Except for me, everyone else here seems able to read one another's mind. But how exactly is that possible? At that very moment I notice Nick exchanging glances with Abba, Abba with Amma, Amma with Luna Apa, and Luna Apa with Amma.

'So, like that.' Nick thinks it over and says, 'Yeah, it's possible.'

Again, I feel Nick is emphasizing the phrase 'like that'. So this is how they read one another's mind, by exchanging glances.

Nick says, 'OK then, one of our team members will be here around 10 a.m. tomorrow. Be ready by then. You can go take a look at the community house today, here's the address. Sanya, don't hesitate to call if you have a problem or need to know something or say something. We're not mind readers, after all.'

Nick smiles. I stare at him, speechless.

4

The doorbell rings at 10.20 in the morning. I've been ready since 8, my suitcase packed. I hear the front door opening and then closing, immediately after which Amma calls out, 'Come downstairs, Sanya, they're here to take you.'

My heart feels heavy suddenly. Surely Amma doesn't want me to go and live somewhere else. I go downstairs with my small suitcase and laptop. Putting them down at the bottom of the stairs, I peep in to find them sitting in the family room. A man gets up when I enter.

'Hi, I'm Steve,' he says, and shakes hands with me.

Me: Hi Steve, I'm Sanya.

Steve: We're here to take you to a community house. Have you packed everything you're planning to take?

Me: Yes, I have. Clothes for two or three days and my laptop.

Amma: Don't you want to take your pillow, baba? You can't sleep without it!

Steve: You may not need to take a pillow, they have pillows.

Me: Not taking it now, Amma, I'll take it later if I need to.

Amma: All right.

Me: Do you know what sort of pillows they have there, Steve?

Steve: I think it must be the regular sort you get in the market.

Me: OK.

Steve: So what's the plan? Do you want me to go on ahead to the community house and you'll meet me there with Sanya?

Abba: Actually, we have no plan. Sanya will go whatever way she wants to, whatever makes her most comfortable. How would you like to go, baba?

Me: I don't think so many people need to go. Let me go with Steve.

Luna Apa: Ok, we'll meet you there in the evening.

Amma: All right, ma, call us when you get there.

Me: OK.

Everyone has come outside to say bye to me. I get into the car. Are those tears in Amma's eyes? The car starts moving before I can check. There's some desultory conversation with Steve but I'm mostly quiet. And besides we reach our destination quite quickly. I get out of the car. Steve gets off too, opens the boot, and takes my luggage out. Pointing to an enormous building, he says, 'So this is the community house. It's huge isn't it?'

'Yeah.'

'Come, let's meet everyone.'

He goes in. I follow with my luggage.

There's no sound inside, it's almost as if there's no one there. Steve knocks on the office door. A girl comes out. 'Hi there,' she says.

'Hi Jo, this is Sanya. Nick's told you about her.'

'Oh yes, our new member at the house. Welcome, Sanya. I'll just get the paperwork done with Steve and then show you around.'

'Sure,' I say, 'I'll wait here.'

Jo leads Steve into the office and comes back in five minutes. 'I'm sorry to have kept you waiting so long,' she says. 'Let me take you to your room first. You can put your things there and then see the rest of the house.'

I agree.

We walk across a large hall, the dining area and the kitchen before taking a corridor on the left to my room, Room No. 6. I don't like it, isn't 6 the Devil's number? At least that's what they showed in *The Omen*.

As these thoughts run through my head, Jo uses a swipe card on a lanyard to unlock the door to my room. Then she hands it to me, tells me to wear it around my neck, so that it's with me when I leave the room. I do as she says and enter.

As I enter, there's a wardrobe on the right facing the door and, right next to it, a small desk fixed quite high up on the wall, with a high chair. High up on the wall opposite is a narrow length of window through which nothing but a slice of the sky is visible and a section of an old church across the fence. A double bed stands close to this wall, almost touching it, with a bedside table on each side. One has a table lamp on it and the other, a radio alarm clock. Near the foot of the bed is a coffee table and a tub chair. A fine arrangement, all told.

Depositing my things in the room, I go out again with Jo to see the rest of the house. She takes me everywhere, shows me the location of the bathroom, the toilet, the music and relaxation room, the place for plates and glasses, where the food is laid out, the lawn in the backyard, the smoking area. Then she says, 'No one's in now, this might be the best time for you to study. Once everyone's back there'll be quite a lot of noise, you may not be able to concentrate.'

I say, 'OK, I'll study, but where's everyone gone so early in the morning?'

Pointing to a sheet of paper tacked up on the wall, Jo says, 'That's the activity timetable. Today's slot says Ikea breakfast, which means they've walked to Ikea for breakfast, they'll walk back afterwards.'

Me: Got it.

Jo: These activities aren't compulsory, but it's good to participate in them.

Me: OK, let me do some reading now.

Jo: Of course. Call me if you need anything.

'OK,' I say and go into my room. Taking 50 cents from my purse, I use the phone booth outside my room, on the right, to call home and tell them I've arrived safely. Back in my room, I ponder over whether to take out my laptop. Then I think I'm not going to be able to get much work done now, why not write in my diary instead. I open the notebook with the picture of the orange and black butterflies that Luna Apa has given me. In it I write:

> I think I'll always remember this day. The CATT has brought me to a community house on Bettina Street. A very large building. Apparently, lots of people live here. I don't mind what I've seen of it so far. The kitchen is probably renovated, but much else here is quite old. The furniture in my room, for example. This chair I'm in is not easy to use, to get into or to get out of. The bed seems too soft. Everything smells like it's old, the kind of old that has no memories attached to it, only a much-used old that's been left behind in the way of others.

Shutting my diary, I climb down from the chair. There's a knock on the door.

Adjusting my veil, I open the door to find Jo standing outside. 'They're returning in ones and twos,' she says, 'come, meet everyone.' Trying to look confident, I say, 'OK.' But I can feel my heart thumping. 'And how do you get to know someone?' I ask myself, and then answer, 'You ask their name.'

Me: And then?

Me: You have to tell them your name too.

Me: After that?

Me: You have to tell them what you do and ask them too.

Me: But I have a feeling many of the people here don't do anything officially, just like me.

Me: Then should I ask about what they used to do?

Me: No, I don't think so. Most of them wouldn't like to talk about their past.

Me: What to do then? I could ask what they'd like to do, but maybe some of them wouldn't like to reveal so much during the very first conversation.

Me: Never mind, let's see what happens.

Stepping into the hall, I find a young guy making tea in the kitchen. He smiles at me. I go up to him and say, 'Hi, I'm Sanya.'

He says, 'And I'm Michael. Did you just get in?'

Me: Yeah.

Michael: Tell me what I can do for you. Can I make you a cup of tea?

Me: Don't bother, I can make it myself.

Michael: Then let me show you around the house.

Me: You don't have to waste so much time for me.

Michael: Not a waste of time at all, come with me. Has Jo shown you around already?

Me: She has, but I don't remember everything.

Michael: No worries, I'll show you everything again.

Michael takes me on a tour of the house, then says, 'Let me know if you have any problems or need anything. My room is next to the art room. I'm an artist, you see, so it helps to be next door.'

'I must see your art sometime,' I tell him.

'Of course,' says Michael.

I can hear conversation and laughter as I step into the hall again. I realize some of the other occupants are back. In the kitchen, three girls are cutting and chopping something, probably following a recipe. Going closer, I say 'hi' to all of them.

They look at me for a moment and exchange glances before returning busily to whatever it is they were doing. 'Can I be of help?' I ask. One of them says, 'John and you can make some salad if you like. The salad things are all in that bag.'

I assume that the only male in the room, more than six feet tall, dressed in a red T-shirt and built like a bodybuilder, is John. Going up to him, I say, 'Hi John.' He doesn't answer. The girl with the air of a leader, whom everyone else refers to as Anne, goes up to John.

'What do you want to slice for the salad?' she asks him. 'Tomato and capsicum,' he says. Anne tells me, 'You can slice the carrots and cucumbers.' I say, 'OK.'

John picks up a knife of his choice and draws a cutting board towards himself. I take the other cutting board and another knife. Glancing towards John as I slice the carrots and cucumbers, I see him slicing tomatoes with rapt attention and mumbling to himself. Is he scolding someone? I remember Dexter the serial killer whom I've seen on TV. It sends a chill down my spine. Who is this John? Who for that matter are all these people?

I finish my work quickly. As I say bye to Anne, she asks, 'Are you Muslim?' When I say I am, she says, 'OK, you can rest now, I'll call everyone when the cooking's done.' 'OK,' I say and go back to my room.

Maybe I'll feel better after a nap, I tell myself. I lie down, but the bed and pillow are so soft that I can't sleep. Besides, I can hear strange sounds from the church on the other side of the fence. I open the window to make better sense of what I can hear. It sounds mostly like Old English or Latin. I can't understand any of it, but it sounds like an incantation of some kind. Whoever it's meant for is repeating some of the sentences. There are also intermittent groans, as though someone's being tortured.

What's going on over there? It can't be an exorcism, can it? Wait, my room number is 6, what if they try something like this on me in a day or two?

Someone knocks several times on my door. 'Coming,' I say and open it. It's one of the girls who were helping Anne with the cooking. Smiling, she says, 'The cooking's done. All of us will eat together now. Come.' I say, 'Good news, I'm starving.' She smiles again. I ask her name. 'Mary,' she says.

Quite a few people have started eating. In the kitchen area, Anne is serving the chicken parmigiana she has made. The aroma pervades the entire building. I ask Anne what she's put in it. 'Chicken and parmesan cheese,' she says. I sit down with my plate. Forks and knives have already been put on the table. I start eating my chicken parmigiana with some salad.

After a few mouthfuls it appears to me there's more beneath the chicken than just cheese. Again, I ask Anne whether she's added anything besides chicken and cheese. She says, as though she's suddenly remembered, 'Oh yes, there's some ham too. You don't eat ham?' I say, 'No.' Mary says, 'Oh no, then you won't be able to eat at all.' I say, 'No problem, I'll have the salad.'

When I start on my salad, Michael stops eating to ask Anne, 'Didn't you know Sanya is a Muslim?' Anne says, 'Yes I did, but I didn't know Muslims don't eat ham.' Michael says, 'I think Sanya deserves an apology from you, Anne.' Anne says, 'An apology for not knowing? OK, I apologize for not knowing.'

Michael stops eating and leaves the table. So do I. And so do several others. Those who remain burst into laughter as soon as we disappear from sight.

Back in my room I sit down in the tub chair. The incantations are still going on in the church. What can I do now? I can write on my computer, but I don't feel like it. Read something? Don't feel like that either. Actually, there's nothing I feel like doing. If I were home, we'd probably be chatting together, then I'd listen to some music. As I think about that, there's a knock on the door.

I open it to find Jo standing outside. She tells me, 'Your family's here to visit you. They're waiting in the dining space.'

When I go there, I see Amma, Luna Apa and Abba sitting at one end of the table. All of them say the community house is beautiful, they like it very much. 'Yes, not bad,' I say. Abba isn't talking much, he's just looking at me. Amma asks me whether I ate in the afternoon. 'I did,' I say, 'but not much.'

Pulling a bowl out of her bag, Amma says, 'There's some rice, your favourite prawn with long melon and fried pumpkin here. Eat.'

I start eating, only to find Abba still gazing at me. Perhaps he's looking at the card slung around my neck. Then he says, 'That card hanging from your neck suits you, you look professional.' I take the card off and slam it down on the table. Still Abba keeps staring at me. I ask him if he wants to share my food. 'No,' he says. It seems he's looking into my eyes to read what's on my mind. I move to the other side of the table. Abba is about to turn towards me, but Amma signals to him not to.

They chat for some more time, then leave. Walking them to the front door, I find a whiteboard next to it, with details of those who have gone out and how long they will be away. After the family leaves, I ask Jo, 'May I also go out for a couple of hours?' Jo says, 'Of course. Just write down where you're going, and how long you'll be away.' I fill in the details and set off towards Monash University.

Although it's summer, there's such a strong wind outside that I feel a little cold. There's almost a storm blowing, a branch from a tree could break and fall on my head any moment. Still, this freedom that I've got is precious. To celebrate, I buy two small packets of chips and a chocolate from a roadside fuel station. When I'm very close to Monash University, I decide not to go there after all. I turn back towards the community house.

When I return, there's no one in the hall, kitchen or dining area. Not even Jo. I don't feel like wracking my brain over where they may have gone. Still, I take a look at the activities and events timetable and realize they're at a community meeting.

I go to my room and lie down. As a variety of thoughts range through my mind, I fall asleep at some point, I don't know when.

I wake up exactly at 8 p.m. As soon as I realize where I am, I leap out of bed. Slinging the card around my neck, I set off for the dining hall. In the kitchen, several people have finished eating and are loading the plates in the dishwasher. Quite a few are eating jam, Nutella, peanut-butter-and-honey sandwiches at the dining table. Possibly this is what dinner is tonight. I make myself a peanut-butter-and-honey sandwich too, eat it at the dining table, put my plate in the dishwasher and settle down in front of the TV in the hall. I usually don't like watching TV, but it's my only connection with my family back home at this time of the day.

I get up after some time. Which is when I realize that there's nobody in the hall or dining or kitchen area besides John, another girl and me. Even Jo is not to be seen anywhere. Meanwhile, the door between the front door and the phone booth is wide open. Something must be going on.

I knock on the office window. An unfamiliar, pretty face opens it and says, 'Hi, what can I do for you?'

'Where's Jo?' I ask.

'Jo was on the day shift,' she says, 'she's gone home. I've replaced her for the night shift. My name is Leonie.'

Me: How do I know who you are?

Leonie: Here's my card. It says here I work here as a support worker.

Me: OK, then I can tell you.

Leonie: Tell me what?

Me: I think something's going on here. Look, both the doors that lead outside are wide open. It seems there's going to be a mishap here any moment, a robbery or murder or kidnapping.

Leonie: Let's hope nothing like that takes place. The doors are open to make it easier for us to move our stocks in. A truck is on its way. Have you seen our storeroom?

Me: No.

Leonie: Never mind, no need to see it now. Let's go to the music and relaxation room instead.

Me: What use will that be?

Leonie: Your fear and anxiety will be dispelled.

Me: I don't want to.

Leonie: Please come, even if it's only for two minutes.

I go to the music and relaxation room with Leonie. It seems to me she might be associated with a criminal gang. Maybe she'll keep me busy here while doing what she has to. Then she'll kidnap or murder me. Even as these thoughts run through my head, Leonie puts on a CD of relaxing music. I let my body and limbs go limp, my eyes close on their own. I overcome my anxiety and fear and return to some sort of calm. I thank Leonie and leave the room. She doesn't say anything.

From one end of the hall I see John doing the dishes at the other end, in the kitchen area. The girl who was here earlier is gone. I feel scared to go anywhere near John, but I manage to run past the kitchen area, my eyes practically closed.

Opening my door quickly, I inadvertently bang it shut and start heaving. There's no comfort in the room either, anyone can shoot me through the window if they want to.

I leave my room again and almost run to the phonebooth. I dial 000 and tell the police everything in detail. The police asks to speak to Leonie. I don't know what they talk about, but when she tells me it wasn't right of me to call the police, I begin to suspect her again. I start trembling with fear and weeping. 'Why are you crying?' asks Leonie. 'Can I do something to make you feel better?'

'I don't feel safe here,' I say. 'I want to go back home.'

'Do you trust me?' she asks.

I don't say anything.

Leonie: If you trust me, you must know that I won't harm you.

Me (somewhat reassured): OK.

Leonie: You couldn't concentrate on your studies at home, am I right?

Me: Still, there can be arrangements at home. Maybe I'll go to the library every day.

Leonie: All right, you can go home if you want to. But will there be anyone to take you home at this hour? It's 10 p.m.

Me: My sister is probably awake. I think I have her phone number in my file. I can take a cab too. I have money for the fare, I have our house keys.

Leonie: No, I'm not letting you take the taxi in this condition. Sit here, I'm going to call your sister.

I sit on the three-seater in front of the TV. When the sofa creaks after a while, I look fearfully to my left out of the corner of my eye to find John sitting at the other end. My heart is beating so fast I feel it will explode. I'm more or less certain I'll be killed now. Trembling and weeping, I fix my eyes on the front door and recite the kalema. Eventually I stand up, unable to take it any more. I pace up and down in the small space enclosed by the sofas, crying.

Suddenly Luna Apa's face floats up in the darkness outside the open door. Swept away in smiles and tears, I sit down on a sofa to compose myself. Soon Luna Apa and Leonie come up to me. Leonie says bye, I thank her profusely. After putting my luggage in the boot of Luna Apa's car, I see Abba and Amma have come too. I smile.

'How're you doing, ma?' they ask.

'I'm fine,' I say.

5

Immediately after the lights blink off and on, the bell rings, sounding something like me-fa-sol-la-ti. An announcement on the loudspeaker says that the library will close in 20 minutes, that the loan desk will remain open for another 10 minutes.

The book I'm reading is from the reserve section, which means I can't take it home. I have to read as much as I can in the next 20 minutes and take notes accordingly.

Vygotsky writes in the introduction to *Thought and Language* that the relationship between these two has not yet been systematically explored. What does Vygotsky mean here by 'systematically'? What do the paradigms preceding Vygotsky discuss? The theories of Marxism and social constructionism do resemble Vygotsky's, but they have separated the past and the present, and the individual and the social. Vygotsky sees similarities rather than differences. Is it right to say 'rather than'? The phrase sounds like separation (or it is used when one is denied and another accepted). Vygotsky's 'phases' are not like Piaget's 'stages', though Vygotsky would like to accommodate Piaget's observations within his own conception. Vygotsky's phases are more fluid and unseparated. So perhaps the phrase 'instead of' can be used in place of 'rather than'. But then it is also true that Vygotsky says words do not have only one meaning, that the meaning changes depending on context.

At this stage of my writing the bell rings out shrilly again, followed by the announcement that the loan desk has closed, and that the library will be open for only 10 minutes more. A bunch of boys and girls are streaming downstairs from the upper floors. What's their hurry? There are still 10 minutes to go, and why are they climbing down the stairs together?

'Excuse me, ma'am, are you Sanya?' the security guard asks.

What could I have possibly done? I ask myself, and answer, 'Yes.'

'There's a phone call for you,' he says, holding his walkie-talkie out towards me.

I take the call in astonishment. 'Hello.'

'Sunny ma, where are you? How're you doing?'

Me: I'm at the library, Amma. I'm good, why have you called me here?'

Amma: I'm so worried. Where did you go off without telling anyone? You've been out for so long, you didn't even call to tell us where you are, how you're doing.'

Me: What's there to worry about? Didn't I tell you in the morning I was going to the library?'

Amma: But I worry. Come home, ma.

Me: Coming, Amma.

I walk to the train station from the Caulfield Campus Library of Monash University. It's dark now. Only the bits under the pools of light from the lampposts are visible. Neither the tops of the buildings nor the sky can be cleary seen. I'm enjoying this walk in the cool breeze, but I've arrived at the station.

Taking a seat in the stationary train, I see a little girl and a woman who is probably her mother smiling at me. I smile back.

The girl comes up to me. When I ask her name, she shows me her nail polish.

Her mother says, 'Tell her your name, Amisha.' Saying 'Amisha' softly, the girl runs back to her mother and hides her face in her lap. The mother smiles and says, 'She's feeling shy. Her auntie has put nail polish on her today, she's very excited about it.'

Smiling, I say, 'You look very pretty in your nail polish, Amisha. I'm an aunty too. I have a niece just like you, did you know that?'

Now Amisha smiles twinklingly at me. A little later, her mother hands me a piece of paper, saying, 'My name and phone number. Call me for anything you need.'

I am astonished. Yesterday too a stranger gave me his phone number at Caulfield Station and told me to call if necessary.

We have arrived at Huntingdale Station. I say bye to the mother and daughter and get off the train.

Huntingdale Station is a seven-minute drive from our house. It doesn't take long on foot either. I start walking quickly. Usually, the bus stop near the station is full of people, most of them students at the Clayton campus.

There aren't too many people hereabouts tonight, though there are lots of cars on the road. The shop attached to the fuel station is open too, I comfort myself as I walk along swiftly. I start listening closely to the passing vehicles. They sound normal now, but are their sounds changing with my changing thoughts? So it seems. Anyway, I'll go to the Clayton Matheson Library tomorrow. I'm sure Vygotsky's book will be available there too. I'm still thinking about the book when I reach home.

The door opens as soon as I ring the bell. In surprise I see Abba, Amma, Luna Apa, Ifa all looking at me anxiously.

'What's the matter?' I ask, and Amma starts crying. Then she caresses my face for a long time, before saying, 'Come inside, baba' and drags me in by my hand.

I think she's taking me somewhere to show me something. 'The fish died some time ago, what's there to be upset about now?

Going into the family room, she leads me by the hand to the two-seater and makes me sit on it before sitting down next to me. Controlling her tears, she says, 'Don't go out like this again, baba, all right?'

Me: Go out like what? I told you before I left. I go to the library because I can't study at home. Should I stop studying?

Amma: I didn't say that, you can go. But call home from the library to let us know if you get there safely, which library it is, when you will be home. You don't use a mobile, we can't check on you. Want mine?

Me: No, I don't like mobiles. But why do you have to check on me? Am I committing a crime? I can't keep you informed about everything, I can't plan so much. All my time will go in planning and keeping you informed, I won't get any work done.

Luna Apa: We called the police, then we cancelled after we reached you on the phone. I'll call them now to tell them you're back home.

Amma: Why not do a little less work for a few days? So many of us are so worried about you, doesn't that mean anything to you?

Me: OK, I'll keep Ifa and Luna Apa informed through Facebook.

Amma: All right, now have dinner and go to bed.

In the morning I discover it's a wintry day with dazzling sunshine. A flock of doves is cooing in unison from the neighbours' roof. They seem to be addressing me. I feel low for a moment, I'm reminded of my first psychosis episode. I used to live in South Clayton at the time. As I was making tea one morning, I looked out of the kitchen window to find a flock of doves cooing continuously in exactly the same way from the neighbours' roof. Doves were a rare sight in South Clayton, so it had made me happy to see so many of them together. Recalling that feeling makes me happy in an instant. I shower swiftly and get ready to go to the library, wrapping a light shawl around myself. I need to leave quickly—the morning mood will be lost if I dawdle.

I observe as I go downstairs that the garage door is unlocked. That means Luna Apa has left for her office already. The sandals that Abba and Amma use at home are lying outside their bedroom door, which means they're still asleep. I try to climb down the staircase as quietly as possible, but when I go downstairs Amma calls out, 'Sunny ma.'

Me: Yes, Amma?

Amma: Come here for a moment, baba.

Me (standing near their bedroom door): Yes?

Amma: Are you planning to go out? Have you showered?

Me: Yes, why?

Amma: Just that I was thinking of going out with you.

Me: Going where?

Amma: Anywhere, just for a drive.

Me: But I'm going to the library now, Ma. Maybe we can go out when I'm back?

Amma: Wait a bit then, I'll come with you.

Me: You'll get bored, Amma. I'll be busy with my own work. I can't spend time with you at the library.

Amma: You don't have to spend time with me, I'll read a book with you.

Me: All right, get ready quickly. You can't take your mobile though.

Amma (once she's dressed): I'm ready.

Me: Let's go then.

Amma: Let me just tell your abba.

Me: All right.

Amma: Listen, I'm going to the library with Sunny.

Abba: OK, but take your mobile.

Me: Amma, you can't bring your mobile. Stay at home.

Amma: Listen, she's saying not to take the mobile.

Abba: Luna'r-ma, I'm telling you to take the mobile.

Amma (taking her phone from Abba and putting it in her bag): Let me take the mobile, ma.

Me (walking away): You can stay at home then.

Amma grasps my arm with both her hands, saying, 'Don't go baba, don't go.' I free my arm with a couple of jerks, open the front door and go out, ignoring Amma's ardent pleas.

I stand on the platform at Huntingdale Station. Perhaps because I walked from home, I'm feeling more settled now after all the drama, though I'm wondering whether the last-minute decision to go to Victoria State Library instead of Clayton at Monash is right. It's fine, actually, there's a particular book that should be available there, which I can read and then visit Clayton.

The words 'Safety Zone' are written on part of the platform floor, and covered in diagonal yellow stripes, I don't exactly know why. I stand in the safety zone, there are many others around me. Most of them have mobile phones, which are pointed towards me.

Why are the people of the world so fond of radiation? What do they do with their mobiles all the time? Is it only used for talking, or for other purposes too? Has technology advanced so far as to scan the brain with phone radiation?

I leave the safety zone, and at that very moment, pushing a wall of air into the station, blowing everyone's hair, clothes and scarves, the train approaches. Everyone who's been sitting stands up. The force of the wind increases, I begin to feel good. When the train stops and the doors open, I get in with everyone else. Then the train starts moving again, swaying from side to side. I sway my way to the nearest available seat and sit down.

'Excuse me ma'am, these four seats are reserved for the aged and the disabled,' a uniformed security guard tells me, 'can you kindly take another seat?'

I want to say, there's no one here who needs this seat right now, what harm will it do if I sit here? I can get up if anyone comes. But I'm not in the mood to prolong the conversation, so I say, 'Yes, of course,' and get up.

The train should be full at this hour. Perhaps it is too, and only this compartment is relatively empty. Two three-seaters face each other; I sit down at one end of the unoccupied one. A boy is sitting near the window on the other one, reading. Each of us is sitting on the extreme right of our respective three-seaters.

Oh, but why am I sitting on the right? Do I support right-wing politics by any chance? No, I don't. I shift to the seat on the left-hand side of the three-seater that the boy's sitting on. He shuffles the pages of his book, perhaps to indicate his disapproval. That's true, I'm not an extreme left-winger either. You could say I'm centre-left.

Now I take the middle seat in the empty three-seater. The boy shuffles the pages of his book again. I go back to the seat on the right. I notice that if I move two-and-a-half seats to the left on the seat opposite me, I can occupy the boy's position. He too can move two and a half seats to arrive at mine. Now I get it, this isn't a game of politics, it's chess. And I'm the dark horse, I have to make my moves accordingly.

Getting off the train at Melbourne Central Station, I try to move accordingly, staying at a distance from the crowd. In particular, I attempt while exiting the station to avoid the crowds that gather on the hour near the enormous clock to stare at the dolls that slide out of its belly.

But I cannot. As I walk, it seems the clock itself is moving alongside me. I look to my left for an instant and see that it's 2 minutes to 10. But what is this I see a moment later? Within a second or two, the minute hand moves twice to signal 10 o' clock. Who is doing all this? I look at my watch. How can this be possible? It's exactly 10 by my watch too. I don't want to think about this any more today.

As soon as I step outside the station, I feel myself lit up by the sun. There's music in the air. The state library is directly across the road, and in front of it is the set-up for the music. Who has made these arrangements? Did they know I'd be here today?

I cross the road. The young guy smiles at me as he sings. I feel all these arrangements are just for me, and my being here is nothing but an excuse to appear in public, in front of all these people.

I enter the library. Although I find the book for which I came, I cannot take it home. I sit down and read the introduction, which appears extremely important, alluring and intense. But this is not a book whose entire meaning I can decipher at one reading.

It occurs to me that I might just get the book at Matheson Library at Monash too.

But I don't get it there. A little disappointed, I pull out my diary. I start writing:

> How does an issue vanish from the attention of a nation? Backward, then a little forward and again a little backward, it vibrates like the strings of a sitar before eventually disappearing. A new issue takes its place then, perhaps a politically more correct one. Can problems have correctness? Isn't it the solution that's usually correct? But perhaps the problem is, too. Problems that we can talk about freely are politically correct problems. Sometimes I am afraid. Because I am me, will I disappear soon too?

As I write this last line, a rush of boys and girls come down the library stairs. This time they don't seem to be in a hurry to go home, it seems something has struck them so deeply that they're about to join a protest on the streets. Looking at them with a smile, I leave the library too after a short while. No, I really must write with great concentration for a few days and for that I need temporary accommodation.

But where will I find that? I don't have any money to speak of. In 2009, a security guard had arranged for me to spend a few days on this very Monash University campus. Unfortunately, that was when I had my first episode. I had to be taken to hospital from the campus itself. But I'm not in the same condition now, so there's no reason for anything like that to happen again.

I spend a long time waiting at the security office, then a man in uniform sits down very casually in the seat next to mine and begins talking. 'Hi, I'm Shane.'

Me: Hi Shane, I'm Sanya.

Shane: Have you been waiting a long time?

Me: Yeah, quite long.

Shane: Do you study or work at this university?

Me: No, neither, though I used to study here. I worked as a tutor too.

Shane: I see. What do you do now?

Me: Officially nothing at the moment. I'm studying on my own, which is why I'm here.

Shane: What are you studying?

Me: Psychology.

Shane: Ah OK. My wife's studying psychology too, she's doing her PhD in developmental psychology.

Me: Wow, really? I was doing my PhD in developmental psychology too.

Shane: So is your PhD done?

Me: No, I couldn't complete it.

Shane: Yes, a PhD's a very difficult business.

Me: I couldn't complete it because of I fell ill.

Shane: Most unfortunate. If you don't mind, can you tell me what the matter was?

Me: It's a long story.

Shane: I have plenty of time.

Me: I had psychosis, in 2009.

Shane: How much progress had you made on your PhD by then?

Me: I was half done. I'd just got through the confirmation-of-candidature stage. I was about to start my research after getting approval from the ethics committee when the illness struck.

Shane: I'm so sorry, that's very sad. Why do you think you developed psychosis though? Was it the pressure of the PhD or something else? Am I asking too many questions?

Me: Oh no, I don't mind talking about it. There was no reason, everything in my life was perfect. I had such a fascinating project for my PhD that nothing could be imperfect, really.

Shane: What was the topic of your PhD?

Me: How self-conscious emotions emerge and develop in children.

Shane: How *do* they?

Me: That's what I'm still trying to understand.

Shane: OK. Now tell me what you're doing here.

Me: Oh, I'm here for my project. I need accommodation for a few days, so that I can work on my project and some related matters. I'm just not able to work at home.

Shane: But this is a security office.

Me: Yes, but it was this office that arranged accommodation for me last time.

Shane: When was that?

Me: In 2009.

Shane: At the time of your psychosis?

Me: Yes, that was when I was hospitalized.

Shane: You were a student here then, weren't you?

Me: Yes.

Shane: And a staff member too?

Me: Yes.

Shane: But not any more.

Me: No.

Shane: You won't get help with accommodation from the security office any more. (Points to a spot on the university map)

But you can go there and ask for help, they can tell you what to do. Or you can come with me, if you trust me, that is. I can help you.

I decide to trust Shane. He makes me climb into an ambulance. I'm not particularly worried by the word 'ambulance' on the side of the vehicle. All I think is, Shane works as a paramedic, he could easily be driving around in an ambulance, it doesn't necessarily mean it's only to take people to the hospital. But as it turns out, he does take me to Monash Hospital.

Instead of making me sit in the large waiting room outside Emergency, he takes me to a smaller waiting room inside. Because it's adjoining the nurses' station, you can often get their attention quickly. But not today. There are fewer nurses, and the one on duty has to go somewhere, so she's closing the nurses' station.

I shift to the large waiting room. Shane and the girl with him ask if I'm comfortable. When I say I am, they leave, telling me someone will attend to me soon.

I sit there for a long time, but no one comes to check on me. I hold a conversation with myself in my head, I try to work out a puzzle, the puzzle of where the double zippers on the paramedics' uniforms begin and where they end. Immediately afterwards, one of the five other people waiting with me gets up and leaves, then another, then yet another, I have no idea why.

I ask myself if there's any reason to keep waiting. No one's shown up yet. I inform the receptionist and leave.

Going out on the main road, I take the bus to the Caulfield campus of Monash University. When I get off there, it feels like a homecoming. I walk directly into the library and get quite a bit of reading done. Afterwards I take a train from Caulfield Station and get off at Huntingdale. I walk home and ring the bell; Abba opens the door.

I go upstairs to my room. I've just about got out of my sweaty clothes and put on a fresh set when the doorbell rings.

Luna Apa is saying in an agitated voice, 'The police are here for Sanya, she left Emergency without telling anyone. Sunny, come out, Sunny, come out!'

Possibly no one can hear that I've been saying 'coming' repeatedly. I go out to discover the police there, and everyone smiling. Ifa enters with a smile too. Are these people only disguised as the police? And is everyone smiling in joy because they won't take me to jail? Where will they take me then? I go down the staircase with all these thoughts running through my head.

As soon as I go downstairs, one of the police officers says, 'Give your mother and sisters hugs.' I hug them obediently.

'Give them kisses on their cheeks too,' the officer says.

I give them kisses.

Then the officer says, 'We'll take you nicely, we won't put handcuffs on you. Come with us.'

I go with them. It's dark everywhere, but even in the darkness I can see a police station wagon parked in front of our house.

One of the officers opens the boot and shows me video cameras, microphones and speakers inside, informing me that should I try to escape or break something, they will see me and take action accordingly.

I am so informed. I follow their instructions to sit at the edge of the boot and then slide my way backward. The paint has come off the section along which I slide, revealing the metal underneath. Who knows how many people have got into this car this way!

The boot closes. It is dark inside. The car starts moving.

6

When the boot opens, I see the car has stopped at Monash Medical Centre. Before I can decide whether to be happy at the sight of a familiar place, I get out of the car on the police officers' instructions. They ask whether I'm OK, and I tell them I am. Then they lead me inside through the main door instead of through Emergency.

But why have we turned to the right? That's where the psychiatric ward is. Of course, there must be examples in history of those who, in an effort to protect their non-mainstream alternative thinking, pretended to be who they were not in order to shield themselves from politics. This may be a similar arrangement. Even as I'm wondering about this, a wheelchair emerges from somewhere and I am told to sit in it. I refuse, saying I'd rather walk. They say if I don't sit in it on my own, they will make me. So I sit.

The wheelchair proceeds down the long corridor. I am flanked by the two police officers, and behind me is the person pushing the wheelchair. At the far end of the corridor are automatic doors with heavy glass panes. I can smell of medicine as soon as we stop in front of them. The tall doors open with a buzzing sound, like an electric shaver. I am overcome by fear for a moment. Where have they brought me? What will they do with me? Are they going to drug me and make me sleep? Will they give me electric shocks?

Meanwhile, the wheelchair stops in front of another set of doors. I remember being here before, during my first episode. A police officer tells someone over the intercom that we are at the door. Someone comes and opens it. Everyone enters. Inside, one of the officers asks me to get out of the chair. The officer hands me my bag, then all of them leave. Slinging the bag over my shoulder, I go to Reception. I'm told they haven't finalized my room yet, that they'll let me know when it's ready. I can wait in the TV lounge till then.

I don't watch much TV. So I pace up and down with small steps, my head bowed, wondering what my time here will be like. Suddenly two young guys come running up from two sides of the square corridor, fold their arms and stand in front of me, their muscles and their shoulders perfectly aligned with each other's as they start to laugh. I can't help but laugh along. One of them holds out his hand to shake mine, saying, 'I'm Glen.' At once the other one does the same, saying, 'I'm Michael.' I tell them my name too, and shake hands. I feel much lighter.

Glen: Nice to meet you, Sanya. How do you like your new home? Ha ha, Just kidding. You won't have to stay here very long, the days will pass before you know it. Come, let me show you around your home.

Me: No need. I've been here before, this is a square-shaped corridor.

Glen: Still, there must have been some changes you don't know of.

I go with them. They wander around, pointing to the artworks and photographs on the walls and commenting on them. I like their analysis. I see no abnormalities of any kind, why are they here? Are they also trying to shield themselves from society and politics by taking refuge in this temporary accommodation called the psychiatric ward? I think the most unusual people in the city are in this ward. It's a unique opportunity for me to learn about them—who knows, we might be able to contribute to one another's work.

I ask Glen about his profession. He says he's a carpenter. I am reminded of my high-school woodwork classes in Year Nine. It needed enormous effort and several weeks to make a wooden bird. What use can Glen's skills be put to in our group? To build houses and furniture in a desolate forest somewhere? I don't think so. We can instead consider carpentry a mixture of labour, diligence and creativity, so it can be useful wherever deep, innovative and analytical thinking is required.

I am startled by a hand on my shoulder.

Glen: Sorry, I didn't want to scare you. I called you by your name several times but you didn't respond, so . . .

Me: No, I wasn't scared, but yes, I have this habit of getting lost in my thoughts.

Glen: Ah, I see. It must be very liberating.

I smile instead of answering. The word 'liberating' swirls about in the confined air.

Glen: So, the reason I was calling you. This is Chris. Superb guitarist. And claims to be a great scientist too.

Me: Is that so? What sort of science do you work on, Chris?

Chris: Physics, biology, chemistry, everything.

Me: All right.

Chris: And mathematics.

Me: Oh, mathematics too?

Chris: Yes. One plus one is not always two. It can also be three—father, mother and the baby. Listen, if you don't mind, may I go now? I have some things to do.

Me: Of course I don't mind. Go ahead.

Glen and Michael continue walking along the corridor with me after Chris leaves, introducing me to the curious faces lining the doors on either side. Most don't seem to have any particular problem. One of them though is mumbling to himself, and his speed increases at the sight of me. He throws something invisible at me over and over again. Perhaps he knows magic. He must have taken a dislike to me and is trying to destroy me with his spell. But that won't be easy because I'm here to serve Allah.

A little farther down I run into another person who probably doesn't like me either. As soon as we get near his room, he unzips his trousers and lets his penis hang out. I look at him. He's so handsome even at 60 or 65 that it makes me wonder how he must have looked when he was young. Is that a wounded resentment blazing out of his deep blue eyes? What is he rebelling against? I look away. In a commanding voice, Michael says, 'Behave yourself, Mick.' Mick retreats into his room at once.

Michael: Please don't be upset. He does these crazy things, but he has a beautiful heart. Give him a day or two, you'll see what a lovely person he is.

Me: I've seen it already.

Glen and Michael laugh.

Glen: Yes, many of the girls are crazy about him.

Me: They need an excuse to be here, after all.

Glen and Michael laugh again. A nurse calls out for me.

My room is ready, a very nice room. A small single bed, a desk attached to the wall on one side and with a chair, and a bedside table and shelf on the other. The bathroom has to be shared with my neighbour. What I'm most relieved about is not having to share a room. From what I've seen, there's very little personal space in shared rooms, and no desk. So you're supposed to just go to your room and fall asleep, provided there's no visitor, of course. I wash my hands and face and go to bed.

In the morning I am woken up by a clatter. Opening the door, I find four men and women in chefs' uniforms pushing two trolleys laden with trays towards the dining hall. The sight makes me hungry. After a quick wash, I head to the dining hall.

Several people are in queue for their trays. Many others are waiting for the queues to become shorter. I sit down too, on the only green sofa in the dining hall.

The queue is getting shorter now. The nurses are holding trays and calling out our names. I go up and wait at the side. None of the trays has my name, since I didn't order a meal last night. They put a tray together for me from the extra food. I sit down in a corner of the square sitting arrangement, and see Glen and Michael approaching with their trays. I wave at them, they smile. Because there's no room beside me, they sit across the table, facing me. As always, I pour corn flakes into a bowl while talking to myself. At once, several people leave the table, including Glen. I glance at their trays to find they were eating Weetabix. I can't tell what's going on, so I pour milk over my cereal and begin to eat.

A girl says 'What nonsense,' and leaves the table, followed at once by several others. I don't feel like eating any more. I am reminded of home, of late the same thing had been happening there too. There were various kinds of food, but the moment I tried to eat any of it I sensed their irritation and heard their sarcastic comments. Has any of this really happened, or is it just in my head?

Putting my tray on the trolley, I join everyone else in the smokers' courtyard. This was not in fact a smoking zone, there are large signs in several places saying 'No smoking in this area.' But people do need somewhere to smoke, so this courtyard was meant for that purpose, and for anyone who wanted to go outdoors. A flock of pigeons flies off to settle on the roofs around me as soon as I open the door. The sound of their beating wings makes me feel good. Everyone is chatting and rolling cigarettes. I seek out a bench at a distance from the smokers and sit down. At once the clouds part and the sunlight falls on my face. The smokers go back inside after finishing their cigarettes, some to play pool, some to watch TV in the lounge. I go to my room to jot down some of my thoughts in my diary.

Luna Apa gave me this notebook, it's a beautifully bound volume, with pictures of butterflies on the front and back. I've written many things in it already, most of them in the form of full sentences and descriptions. I was thinking of demonstrating some things with mathematics, but I'm not sure whether that would be right. I had begun solving a mathematical problem in the library, before coming to the hospital. I couldn't work it out eventually, I think I made a mistake at the beginning with the formula. But I'm trying to move away from formulae, why did I use one then? Was it just to explain it to everyone? Why do I have to explain anything to anyone? They will learn my language on their own if they want to. Even as these thoughts run through my head, I hear an uproar outside and go out.

A middle-aged man near Reception is asking everyone whether they have 50 cents, and saying, 'Father Moran will visit me tomorrow, he'll take me away, I'll get to meet my brothers.'

'That's good news, Dominic,' says everyone. 'We understand, now calm down.'

Glen is the only one talking to him nicely and answering his questions politely. Spotting me in a corner of the reception area, Dominic comes up to me to ask, 'Do you have 50 cents?'

'What'll you do with 50 cents?' I ask him.

'I'll call Father Moran,' he says.

Exuberantly he adds, 'Father Moran is coming to take me away tomorrow. I'll get to meet my brothers.'

I say, 'Just a minute, let me get you 50 cents.'

I bring 50 cents from my room and hand it to him. He's delighted. He asks me my name, and I tell him.

On the way back to my room, I think about how everything might be fine, but the mystery of why everyone suddenly went off into the courtyard and then returned after they had smoked their cigarettes has not been solved.

I see Glen going into the TV lounge with a bottle of water. I follow him in there, and sit down next to him. When I ask him why everyone went into the courtyard, he shows me the bottom of the water in his bottle, where I see some white grains. 'Arsenic,' I think to myself in bewilderment, and look at Glen with wide eyes. So it was to protest against this that everyone went into the courtyard. So the courtyard is a place for protests. How active! How romantic! I seize Glen's hand without even knowing it. My own hand is shaking. Putting the bottle on the floor, Glen squeezes my hand with both of his.

Later, Glen races up when I'm walking in the corridor in the evening and then slides on his knees till he reaches me. 'This is for you,' he says. He's disappeared before I can find out what he has brought me. I unclasp my fingers to find a white daisy in my palm. It fills me with joy. I walk along the corridor with my flower when I run into Michael. 'Glen is leaving tomorrow,' he says. 'Where is he going?' I ask. 'Home?' Michael says, 'To a community house, perhaps.'

'I see,' I say, and resume walking. I need some fresh air. As soon as I open the door to the courtyard, all the pigeons fly off again. Gusts of wind make my hair blow, my blurred vision grows sharp again. Once more the clouds part to let the sunbeams light up my face.

Whose melodious voice is that? And how beautifully someone's playing the guitar.

They're occupying the two benches in the middle, with Daniel, Mick and Dominic on one, and Glen next to them on the ground, and Michael and some others on the bench opposite theirs, which is why they haven't seen me come in. Who knows when Michael came out here! Glen is looking straight at me and singing with a big smile. Dominic is also singing with his eyes on me. There's so much passion in his voice, and Michael is playing the guitar so well—I flash them a smile. Dominic is singing:

When I find myself in times of trouble
Mother Mary comes to me . . .

7

There's a shooting pain in my head. I don't know what time it is or how long I've been sitting this way. My entire body feels numb. My eyes are fixed on the darkness outside the large window. I could see three trees as long as there was daylight, the leaves they had shed were gathering in ones and twos at their feet. Falling off the branches to which they had clung lovingly, they added to the pile of leaves like children gathering at an orphanage. Then a gust of wind scattered them; whatever refuge they had from one another was lost. Now all they had was themselves, along with the wind and its whims.

Where will it take me, this wind, this system? Glen has probably gone to a community house somewhere. And I couldn't spend even a single night there. Is the community house better than the hospital? Maybe. At least it allows something like the 'self' to exist, something like 'me', something like 'want'. If I want to go out somewhere of my choice, all I have to do is write the details of where I'm going and when I'll be back. I can eat the food of my choice at any restaurant that I want. I can let myself grow through the internet and computers, on the pages of books, with my work. To be sure, there are restrictions, taking medication is compulsory there too, but these obligations are much more relaxed. Still, could they be more dangerous for that very reason? Is it like the unprotesting death of the frog in a pot of slowly heating water?

On the other hand, no such thing as 'self' is allowed to thrive here in this hospital. You're not allowed to bring your computer. You cannot use the internet, or find books and articles of your choice. You cannot find yourself in others either, for there is no assurance of how long anyone will remain, or where they will be, and when. The self is subdued with medication at every opportunity.

I feel like weeping again. The entire day has passed this way—crying . . . sitting still . . . then crying again. But I haven't budged an inch since I sat down here. The afternoon has given way to evening, evening to dusk, dusk to night. My eyes have been fixed outside the window all the time. There have been storms outside throughout, the state of my mind matching the state of nature to provide some sort of consolation. I have been weeping ceaselessly to this comfort, saying to myself, 'Wasia kursiyuhus samawati wal ard'—His chair extends over heaven and earth.

I had run off towards Reception when they forced me to take an injection. Let alone scream and shout, I couldn't even say much in protest. So I could only weep, saying how unfair they had been to me, how cruel they were. Wendy at Reception scolded me, 'Go to your room, Sanya, go to your room at once.'

Me (crying): I won't, I won't. Tell me first why you're torturing me, I've done you no harm.

Bodybuilder Russell (echoing Wendy): You don't understand, Sanya, you're not well.

About to answer him, I couldn't summon the words to my lips, I burst out crying and looked away in rage and humiliation. This same Russell had refused to leave my room earlier when I was being given the injection in my buttocks. It was only when I said that come what may, I would never take my clothes off in his presence, that Jane had made him leave. So I began to bristle when he said it wasn't he but I who was not well. I sat on the floor with my back to the Reception wall, my legs splayed out, crying. Jed came running out of his room.

Jed: What's the matter, Sanya, why are you crying?

Me (weeping:) I feel I've been raped. The needle wasn't a needle but something else.

Nurse Brenda (who was passing by): Don't be so deluded, you were merely given an injection, nothing more.

Me: But all of you ganged up and insisted that I take the injection. You said you'd literally force me. It's my body and I have never done you any harm. You're coercing me. (My words end in a shout.)

Brenda: Listen, you need to calm down. Should I give you some mood stabilizers?

Another bout of crying. A perplexed Jed went off towards the courtyard, and I came to my room and sat down on the bed. It has just occurred to me that I've been sitting here ever since then.

It's unnaturally silent here. Yes, it's late, but not all that late. I was starving earlier, I hadn't eaten all day, but my hunger has vanished now. My body feels numb all over.

The first thing I do when I come out of the bathroom is to go to Reception to check the time. There are two clocks there, one on the wall and one on the front desk. The table clock displays the day and date too. Both the clocks say it's 10 p.m., so I assume that's the correct time. But are the day and date correct? I don't know, no one tracks dates or months here. Even time is tracked only in terms of breakfast, lunch and dinner. Reflecting on this, I realize my throat is parched.

I am greeted with a loud welcome as I walk into the dining room.

Jed: We're having pizza, Sanya. Come join us.

Me: Thank you, Jed, but I don't eat ham. Let me check for sandwiches in the fridge.

So many people eating pizza at this hour of the night. Does this mean they haven't had dinner either? Are they protesting? On my behalf?

I gulp down several glasses of water, then take a salad sandwich out of the fridge and sit down at one end of the table to eat it. Like me, several others are also eating sandwiches of different kinds. There are separate baskets of tea, long-life milk, sugar, fruit and cookies in the kitchen. Finishing my sandwich, I help myself to some single-serve crackers from the kitchen, return to my seat and start stuffing them into my mouth. Chewing hard, I look up to discover Frank, wearing his sunglasses on his head, gazing at me with his compassionate, beautiful blue eyes. When our eyes meet, I burst into tears, my mouth still full of crackers. And I see tears in the eyes of the 60-year-old Frank despite his tough-guy image.

I get to my feet. I'd have liked some fresh air, but that's impossible, the windows here can't be opened. The doors to the courtyard are closed too. I go into the prayer room next to the pool room. Messages from various religions have been put up on the walls. I look at them cursorily before taking a chair in the corner, trying to free my mind of all thoughts for some time. Nothing works. I read suras, cry a little and start to feel a little calmer.

Back in my room, I try to end the day with a beautiful thought of some sort. Has nothing good happened today? Of course it has, just a short while ago in the dining hall. And also, during the day, when I was sitting on my bed, the swaying of the three trees outside, the shedding, gathering and flying of the leaves seemed to have been telling me something. I write about it in my diary.

> Near my hospital window
> Stand these trees.
> I see them and feel at peace
> I know they are close to my soul,
> Even if we are not related by blood.
> Of the three I see from my bed,
> One is evergreen, one coloured in autumn hues,
> And one stands unclothed.
> Like a naked baby—no clothes, no worries either.
> I see them, they remind me of my mother's garden
> Green, colourful, lively
> When it rains there
> Through my window I can see
> How beautifully the squash leaves bathe in the rain.

I wake up after a sound night's sleep. I feel very comfortable, at the same time my head feels hollow. Is the hollowness on account of losing my appetite? I can't tell. It must be quite late, the unnatural silence is back. Is it lunchtime, or has the lunch hour passed? Either way, I don't feel like eating. I'd better go and see where everyone is.

The food trolleys clatter past me as soon as I set foot in the corridor. I step aside to make way. The trolleys go past and on towards the dining hall. I go to Reception to find out what time it is. It's 1.30 on the wall clock, and 12.30 on the table clock. I wait a long time to ask which of them is correct, but everyone is too busy to even spare a glance, let alone talk. I go into the dining hall.

There's a wall clock here as well, which says it's five past one. Something tells me the table clock at Reception showed me the wrong time, it's at least 1 p.m., maybe even 1.30. I'm guessing, of course, but it is my impression that those who pray regularly or those who feel more connected to nature usually get it right when it comes to guessing the time.

Anyway, they usually serve lunch by 12.30. If it's 1 or even 1.30 now, then they're quite late. Why this delay? Is it deliberate? Is it to ensure that everyone eats, that everything is all right? I'm not going to eat, though. I'm not hungry, and I'm not enjoying this bullshit. Walking past the stationary trolleys, I open the door to the courtyard.

I'm a little hesitant about setting foot outside. The pigeons are sitting or standing very close to the door. I love animals and birds but I am afraid to go near them, even though I know they won't hurt me. Gathering all my courage, I put one foot in the gap between two pigeons, whereupon they move away a little to make room. I use the space to walk to a bench and sit down.

The benches in the courtyard are packed, the ground is covered with pigeons too. Chris has put his CD player on speaker mode, playing music for himself and everyone else. He's playing his guitar too sometimes, singing tunelessly now and then, and talking. At one point he begins to cry. He seems terribly lonely to me. I go up to him.

Me: Can I give you a hug, Chris?

Chris: Sure, you can. But keep your chest at a distance.

I keep my chest at a distance and give Chris a hug.

Jed: And me? What about all the trouble I went to for you?

Smiling, I sit down next to Jed and give him a hug too. Among the pigeons wandering around near his feet is Itchy. I believe it's Daniel who has chosen the name. The pigeon is a little smaller than the rest, one of its wings is injured. There aren't too many feathers on its neck and shoulders, and it appears Itchy prefers human company. Of course, many of the pigeons here like to hang out with people. I think they're particularly attracted to the smell of tobacco. Jed gathers Itchy in his arms. When I move a little farther away, he sets the pigeon down.

Jed: Are you afraid of pigeons?

Me: I'm afraid of pigeons, dogs, cats, moths, cockroaches—anything that moves.

Jed: Why?

Me: I don't know. Maybe because they're unpredictable.

Jed: If you look at it that way, even people who move about are unpredictable. But you go up to them easily enough, you comfort them too.

Me: That's true. But I won't go near a serial killer. They could kill me.

Jed: You're frightened of being near birds and animals even though you consider them harmless. It can't be just unpredictability, it must be something else.

Me: Like what?

Jed: Something within you. Think about it.

Me: Could it be the way I was conditioned by my family and society during my childhood?

Jed: I don't know. But from what I've seen of you, you're not exactly the assertive kind, you're quite placid.

Me: What do you mean?

Jed: When Chris was crying, everyone else just sat around, but you felt the need to console him. Because his crying affected you, it made you respond. Or when Dominic asked for money, you gave it to him at once. Why did you?

Me: Empathy?

Jed: I don't think it's empathy in that sense. I think you respond even before you work out what exactly has taken place.

Me: In that case, isn't my consoling Chris or giving money to Dominic when no one did a form of assertiveness?

Jed: You didn't assert yourself with a 'I want this', you reacted keeping in mind what someone else in the situation was wanting or may want.

Me: Maybe.

Jed: It's the same with birds and animals. You maintain a distance from them because you don't know what they want from you, and whether you can or want to give it to them.

Me: Right.

Jed: You can also try asking them for something. They might also want to react to your request.

I stand up with a smile. The pigeons fly off together as soon as I set foot among them. I am not frightened at all. I am filled with joy.

8

I open the courtyard door and step inside. Several people are having lunch. I don't know many of them. While I've seen some of the others sitting quietly in their shared rooms, I've never seen them outside. I don't understand why they have decided to eat in the dining hall today or what its significance is.

I remain steadfast in my decision not to have lunch. Many of the inmates have started coming in from the courtyard. Some of them are sitting down to lunch, the rest are going off towards their rooms. A few go into the kitchen to collect a fruit or a cup of tea or cookies. I get myself a cup of tea and stand in the kitchen with Jed, Chris and others. The tiny kitchen is packed now. A young guy of 27 or 28 pushes through the crowd to come up to me and says, 'Hi, I'm Glen.'

Jed: Oh, so you're Glen Two? Chris has told me about you. You arrived last evening, right?

Glen: Yeah, I arrived last evening, I saw all of you from a distance. I wanted to come up to you but I didn't, the situation didn't seem right. But why am I Glen Two? Where's Glen One?

Chris: Glen One isn't here any more. We don't know where he is, maybe he's at a community house somewhere.

Glen: Oh, OK.

Me: The beginning of my stay at the hospital was very beautiful thanks to Glen One. We couldn't give you a similar environment, I'm sorry.

Glen: Oh, don't be sorry, the environment in this hospital is much better than that of the place I'm coming from.

Me: Where are you coming from?

Glen: Dandenong Hospital.

Jed: I see. You look like you've been through a lot!

Glen: Don't ask.

Me: All right, we won't. But aren't you going to eat lunch? Lunchtime will end soon.

Glen: No, I'm not really hungry. I'll have a cup of tea with you.

All of us smile. The lunch trolleys clatter past the kitchen door.

We finish our tea and head to the TV lounge or to our respective rooms. I stop at Reception to check the time. The wall clock and the table clock are showing the same time now, around 3 p.m. But the table clock says it's Thursday, even though I know it's Friday today. Sister Amira told me the day before yesterday that she wouldn't be on duty on Friday because she was having guests over.

About to enter my room to pray, I see a yellow 'Cleaning in Progress' sign outside. So my room's being cleaned. I have no choice but to go towards the prayer room, but both the pool room and the prayer room are locked. Going into the dining hall, I find the same signboard outside the open door of the kitchen, there's a cleaner at work inside. The door to the courtyard is closed too. Through its glass panes I can see the yard being washed down with jets of water from a hosepipe. A yellow signboard saying 'Cleaning in Progress' stands on my side of the door.

So I have no choice but to walk around the corridor in a circle. Or a square. I discover several cleaners at work in different places. The one who was cleaning the kitchen is now cleaning the second TV room. I take the opportunity to go into the kitchen and help myself to a cookie. One more round, one more cookie. I make several circuits of the corridor, grabbing cookies or crackers each time. At one point, when I go in for one more cookie, I find a bowl of fruits on the cookie box. I look around to discover Aaron leaning against the kitchen benchtop, smiling. I find this very funny. I ask Aaron if it's his doing, and he nods. I take an apple, bite into it and resume walking.

A cleaning trolley is blocking my way at one end of the corridor. The cleaner is spraying something on the wall and wiping it clean. Although the spray has a lemon fragrance, its toxic fumes choke me, numbing my sense of smell and making my throat burn.

Me: Excuse me, may I know your name?

Cleaner: My name is May.

Me: Can you move your trolley a little, May? I need to pass this way.

May: Of course. Just push it, it will roll to one side.

I nudge the trolley sideways and go on my way. May busies herself spraying the wall and wiping it down.

An Asian cleaner is working on another wall in the same way at the other end of the corridor. I say, 'This spray, you know, it . . . '

Before I can finish, the cleaner says, 'Spray?', points the nozzle at me and releases an aerosol near my face from her canister. I move away quickly, I have no idea what made her do this. Did she think I was asking her to spray? Or was this hostility?

Miserably, I go into the TV lounge and sit down in one corner of the three-seater sofa. Suddenly someone says, very gently, 'Hi.'

Me: Oh, hi Glen Two, were you here all along?

Glen: I was.

Me: How come I didn't see you?

Glen: You weren't looking for me.

So Glen Two had been sitting alone in the TV lounge all this while? And that too, without switching on the TV? Was he upset about something? I try to think of something beautiful quickly, a song or poem about friendship that can make him feel better. But nothing comes to mind. Then I remember a few lines from a song. And, without any preparation, I take Glen Two's hand as though we're about to arm-wrestle and say in a quivering voice, 'Never will this friendship . . . '

Putting his other hand on my shoulder, Glen Two says, 'Yes, tell me now.'

Spontaneously I say,

'Never will this friendship break
I might lose my life
But I won't leave your side.'

Kneeling on the floor, Glen Two brings his mouth near our clasped hands and kisses his own hand. 'No one has ever told me anything so beautiful,' he says. I kiss his hand too. Getting back to his feet, Glen Two frees his hand and says, 'Do you know why I kissed my own hand instead of yours?'

Me: Why?

Glen: So that its traces don't remain on you.

Me: Sorry, actually I didn't think . . .

Glen: No worries. Now come with me.

Me: Where?

Glen: To walk a few rounds.

Me: I was walking all this while. I came in here because I couldn't go on.

Glen: OK, you stay here then, I'll go.

Me: No, I'm coming too.

Glen Two and I start walking. The cleaning is still underway. We complete two rounds, and during our third, the cleaner named Ing quietly opens the pool room door and whispers to us, 'You can go in here. If you want to go into some other room, tell me, I have the keys, I'll unlock the door.'

I say, 'Thank you, Ing. Do you think you can unlock the door to the smaller courtyard for us?

Ing (shaking his head): No, I don't have those keys.

Me: Who has them?

Ing: You can try asking at Reception.

Me: You have the keys to all the rooms, but not to the small courtyard? Why?

Ing: They weren't given to me. I think it's because the grass is artificial in there and birds don't sit on it, so it needs no cleaning.

One section of the fence around this courtyard is covered with corrugated tin. Beneath this section is a trench—when rainwater gathers in it, reflections of passing cars appear on the surface. Clearly the main road runs just outside the fence, which means anyone can escape if they try. Perhaps that's why unsupervised entry to this courtyard is not allowed. I don't tell Ing about this, I only walk up to the windows in the dining hall from where the small courtyard is visible, take a seat and reflect on the beauty of the fence. The concrete wall next to the section of corrugated tin is painted with blue and orange waves, like the reflection of the setting sun in the water. When it rains, there's real water in the trench beneath, does this count as magic realism? What kind of person likes magic realism? I might have understood some of this if I'd read up on it. Why did the authorities want to express this on the boundary wall on one side of the psychiatric ward? It is as though this manifestation of magic realism is a boundary between the psychiatric ward and the real world.

I look away from the courtyard and turn my eyes towards Glen Two and Ing. They are standing at the other end of the dining hall, talking to each other and glancing at me occasionally. I stand up and walk over to them. Thanking Ing, Glen Two and I go into the pool room to find Jed, Belinda, Michael and Tammy playing pool in there.

Michael: Heyyyyy, welcome to our world.

Me: What do you mean your world? It's my world too.

Michael: No, it's just that you don't visit the pool room usually, that's why I said it.

Me (smiling): Yes, actually I'm here because I couldn't stick anywhere else.

Glen: Ha ha, just like you checked on me only because you couldn't stick anywhere else.

Me: What do you mean? That was why I went to the TV room, but not why I checked on you.

Jed: In a sense, that too was because you needed to. What did I tell you in the courtyard earlier today?

(Laughing, Jed and Glen give each other high fives. I laugh too.)

Belinda: What are you guys talking about?

Me: Something personal. I don't want to talk about it.

Belinda: What can Jed have that's too personal to tell me? Is he closer to you than he is to me? (Her voice quivers and her eyes fill with tears.)

Me: Oh no, it's my personal matter, not his.

Belinda: No, I've noticed this before too. What is it that she has that I haven't, Jed? Am I not pretty enough? Sexy enough? Smart enough? Articulate enough? What?'

Tammy (adding her voice to Belinda's): What do you guys see in her, Michael, tell us.

I don't want to be part of any of this, so I leave. Glen Two comes out with me too. We start walking again along the corridor, this time slowly, observing the artworks and notice boards on the wall. One of the boards has several 'Before and After' pictures tacked up on it. In one of them, the 'Before' depicts an untidy desk, and the 'After', an orderly one. In another 'Before', the entire room is in a mess, and in the 'After' everything is spick and span. And so on.

I feel the pictures are trying to hint at something over and above personal hygiene. But what? Perhaps they signal ideological as well as lifestyle diversities. Since everything is written in English, the 'Before' is on the left, naturally, and the 'After', on the right.

What are the pictures saying? Keep everything neat and tidy? Why are they saying this? I recall that before coming to the hospital, in fact even before going to the community house, I used to feel some sort of pressure in my head. One day Amma came into my room, picked up the plastic bags and empty packets strewn on the floor and told me to keep the room clean. Even this little act of cleaning up reduced the pressure in my head greatly, not that I know if it was related. If that was the reason, how was it possible?

Pondering over this, I observe the board on the opposite wall. A poster next to it has a picture of a photocopier. On it are the words, 'The best invention of the 20th century is the copy machine'.

I don't quite get this either, all I grasp is that perhaps in the course of an ongoing argument, one side has been compared to photocopiers, its members might be copying other members or making other members copy them.

Walking farther on, all the way to Reception, I find these words painted in large letters on the wall of the corridor leading to the medicine room:

> Working collaboratively to provide
> individualized care that promotes
> wellness and recovery.

What do they mean by 'individualized' here? 'Individualized' from the viewpoint of what kind of social system?

Individuals in a collectivist society might want to unite with one another so profoundly that their self–other boundaries merge as they become aware of one another's extremely personal matters. But this does not mean—indeed, for this very reason—there is freedom in a real sense. In the process of depending upon one another, people may turn into one another. As a result, those who are by nature gentle, or whose 'self' is comparatively undeveloped, are being forced to lose their individuality repeatedly to those who are harsher or have a more developed 'self'. Moreover, not everyone depends on others the same way. Some depend by loving, some out of the inability to do something, some by asserting their power. Love and inability might be considered weaknesses in such societies. The more information someone has about society, its activities and its people, the more powerful they will become and the more they will use that power on the weak. Even if those being considered weak believe in different ideologies which may not consider them weak at all. So this social system is not suitable for those who have low or even no practicality—which is necessary to 'know' something. Such a society will only oppress them. But does it consider that their thinking is in fact much more creative, much more individualized—for they are inspired from within themselves rather than by external factors? Does it realize that these people also need security and care? Is this medication-based, 'collaborative' and 'collectivist' system really doing anything 'individualized' for such people?

Lost in these thoughts, I don't realize when I have arrived outside my room. I look up to see Glen Two smiling at me. I smile too, assuming he's amused at how distracted I am. But when I see what's in front of me, I realize the real reason. My room has been cleaned all right, but someone's sleeping in my bed, beneath my blanket. And the shelves are filled with clothes and things I don't recognize. Worried, I go to Reception and say, 'Excuse me Jane, someone's lying in the bed in Room No. 3. And my things are no longer there.'

Jane: Oh, the room's been allotted to a new patient. You're going to be in Room No. 10 from now on.

Me: And my things?

Jane: Your things are in these three bags (opening a door behind her and handing them over).

Saying goodbye to Glen Two, I go into Room No. 10 with my bags. This one's a beautiful room too, with a view of trees through the window. It's at one end of the corridor, the corridor that runs through the dining hall and past the pool room and the prayer room. I start arranging my things on the shelves when there's a knock on the door. I look up to find an incredibly handsome young guy of 26 or 27 standing there. I can't take my eyes off him.

'May I come in?' he asks.

Me: Of course.

He (stretching out his right hand): May I have 50 cents?

Me: Hee hee, how did you know? Did you see me give Dominic 50 cents?

He: May I have 50 cents?

Me: OK wait, let me check if I have it on me. But first, tell me your name.

He: Ivan.

Me (taking the money out of my purse): Here's 50 cents.

Charmed, I gaze at Ivan standing near the open door, not just because he's handsome but also because he copied Dominic to show his support for him. I see a beautiful person in a beautiful body. Ivan looks at me in a lovely way too, does he also see a beautiful person in me?

At that moment I see that Glen Two has walked up the corridor to my door. His eyes are filled with tears. I sit on one corner of my bed, gazing out the door. Ivan leaves the room. Glen Two walks one round after another along the corridor, his T-shirt drenched in sweat.

9

At lunch they give me a plate piled with salad and prepacked tandoori chicken and rice heated in the microwave. I push the tandoori chicken and rice away, at which the girl on my right says, 'Aren't you eating it? Give it to me then.'

I pass it to her, and at once she opens the packet and begins to wolf it down. Lifting the lid off my plate of salad, I discover my tray doesn't have a fork or spoon. How am I supposed to eat? Even breakfast had been insipid. They were giving Glen Two an injection early in the morning, his hands and feet had been tied. Walking along the corridor, that's how I saw him, he was screaming. They shut the door when they saw me. So I don't exactly feel like eating now, but I must, because I'm starving.

I start eating the salad with my hand. This tray without a fork and spoon is meant to humiliate me, isn't it? I won't be humiliated, I'm used to eating with my hand. Suddenly I find Glen Two sitting opposite me, he's also eating his lunch with his hand.

Me: Oh, it's you, Glen Two. When did you get here? How're you doing?

Glen: I came a while ago. I'm good, I'm always good.

Me: Last night too? When you kept walking round and round the corridor?

Glen: You mean when I was exercising? Yes, I was.

Me: And this morning?

Glen Two smiles. 'Listen,' he says, 'when we get out of all this, I'm going to take you to a good Indian restaurant where everyone eats with their hands.'

'OK,' I say, smiling. At that moment Nurse Ian comes up to Glen Two to tell him the ambulance has arrived, he'll be leaving after his meal.

'Ambulance?' I ask in surprise. 'Yes, I'm being sent back to Dandenong Hospital,' says Glen Two and stands up. I look at him walking away, my vision blurring. My tears drip onto my salad. I keep eating it with my hand.

'May I sit here?' someone asks. I look up to see Ivan with his tray, standing behind the chair where Glen Two was sitting. My heart dances with glee. Smiling through my tears, I say, 'Of course. Please do.'

Ivan sits. He eats with his fork, and I with my hand.

We complete our meals in near silence, and then stand up together. Putting his tray onto the trolley, Ivan goes out to the courtyard. I wash my hands in the kitchen and follow him out, where I see him gathering the cigarette butts strewn on the ground. He asks whether I have cigarettes. I say I don't. Then he asks whether I have a lighter or matches. I don't have those either. Then he gets hold of a lighter from someone else and lights a butt he has picked up. After a drag or two on several butts, Ivan goes back inside and I follow him.

Where do the others get tobacco and cigarette paper? In the medicine room, perhaps? Ivan can easily ask them, why smoke the discarded butts? Why doesn't he ask? Is he trying to quit smoking? Even as these questions run through my mind, I see Ivan strolling down the corridor, his hands clasped behind his back. He's gripping his left wrist with his right hand, and his left hand, which dangles loosely, is swaying in time with his movement. I run up to him and take his left hand. He holds mine tightly. I feel so good, I feel safe. I stand in front of him. He stops and looks at me with his deep green eyes. I put my arms around him and put my head on his chest. He wraps his arms around my shoulders. Suddenly the hospital feels like a wonderful place.

'Sanya!' someone shouts. Startled, I look around to find Nurse Pauline looking daggers at me. I let go of Ivan quickly, and he resumes his walk.

Nurse Pauline: I'm warning you not to follow the boys around any more.

Me: But I don't follow the boys.

Nurse Pauline: You don't? I see you with boys all the time.

Me: How many girls do you have here anyway? And I do spend time with girls too, provided they're the right sort.

Nurse Pauline: You must not follow Ivan around any more.

Me: But he's my boyfriend.

Nurse Pauline: How long have you known him for him to be your boyfriend?

Me: Do you have to know someone a long time for them to be your boyfriend?

Nurse Pauline: I'm not going to argue with you. You're not allowed to follow him around. He doesn't like it.

Me: Has Ivan said he doesn't like it?

Nurse Pauline: He doesn't have to say it, it's obvious. Anyway, Dr Wong wants to see you. Go to Interview Room One at once.

I knock on the door of Interview Room One. 'Come in,' says a voice.

Pushing the door open, I find Dr Wong and Dr Nevin sitting next to each other against one of the walls, and two younger men sitting against another.

Dr Nevin: Sit down, Sanya. So, how're you doing?

Me (taking a seat): I'm doing good, Dr Nevin, how about you?

Dr Nevin: So am I, thanks for asking. Sanya, you know our senior doctor, Dr Wong, don't you?

Me: Yes, I've seen Dr Wong before.

Dr Nevin (pointing to the young men): And these are Leo and Jerry, final-year medical students.

Leo and Jerry smile and wave. I smile and nod in acknowledgement.

Dr Nevin: Can they stay here while we interview you?

Me: Of course.

Dr Nevin: How do you feel in the hospital, Sanya?

Me: Not too good.

Dr Nevin: Are you missing home?

Me: Yes.

Dr Nevin: How do you pass your time here?

Me: It's not easy, I have to force myself.

Dr Nevin: What do you do all day?

Me: Most of the time my day goes well when my family visits me. The rest of the days I spend on self-care, eating, making diary entries.

Dr Nevin: What do you write in your diary?

Me: Whatever comes to mind. Incidents, poems, ideas.

Dr Nevin: Yes, Nurse Nick was saying you think a lot. We'll talk about that some other time. We've called you here today because we're worried about you.

Me: Worried?

Dr Nevin: Yes. For one thing, it seems you don't meet all the members of your family. May we know why? Are you afraid of something?

Me: No, I'm not afraid. It's because I'm upset with them.

Dr Nevin: Upset? Why?

Me: Because they sent me to hospital, and the way they did it. And after packing me off here, they actually come and visit me as though everything is normal.

Dr Nevin: But it was a good decision to send you to hospital, very responsible of them. You should be grateful to your family. You're under proper supervision here, getting proper treatment.

Me: I don't trust psychological treatment in the medical model.

Dr Wong: We do even if you don't. And we believe you need further treatment.

Me: May I know why you think I do?

Dr Wong: The answer to your why brings us to the second reason for being worried, which is your habit of following our male patients around the place.

I jump to my feet, my eyes well up. I say, 'I don't follow them, I'm not a stalker, I become friends with them.'

Dr Wong: Yes, and this friendship makes you intimate with them.

Me: That's not how it is, Dr Wong. Besides, this kind of thing happens outside the hospital too, do you treat them with medication as well?

Dr Wong: Does this mean you're refusing treatment? We were told you didn't want to take your injection the other day, you cried. Your mood isn't stable, you have no control over yourself.

Me: There were reasons to cry that day, psychological reasons beyond physical causation. There's reason to cry today too.

Dr Wong: Lithium! Lithium! Lithium!

They prescribe lithium for me alongside Olanzapine.

Me (crying as I open the door to leave): Why did you call me for an interview if you aren't even going to listen to me? You didn't get me here to discuss anything, your minds are already made up.

Still weeping as I walk towards my room, it occurs to me that I've spent all my tears the day they gave me the injection, all I have left is anger. Or do I? Maybe the only thing left is weariness. I am overcome by waves of exhaustion.

Going into my room, I lie on my back on the bed, my legs dangling over the side. Nurse Vivian appears almost at once to tell me my family is here to see me. I sit up.

Amma comes in, along with Heera Maama, who is holding a bunch of yellow roses. Instead of asking them to sit, I stand up and tell Amma, 'There's not enough room here, let's go sit over there.'

We walk into the prayer room and find Ivan sitting in a corner. It's good to see him there, though I don't express my feelings, I only say 'hi' and introduce him to Amma and Heera Maama. They sit down, and I sit at the other end of the room, facing them.

Heera maama: How're you doing, ma?

Me: I'm good.

Amma: Maama has brought you flowers.

Me: There's no room here for flowers, you'd better take them home. They'll look better there, they'll thrive too.

Amma: Your maama went to so much trouble to get them. I did tell him there's no need, but he insisted.

Heera maama: We could ask at Reception if they'll let you keep the flowers.

Me: No need, maaama, please don't mind, take the flowers home.

Heera maama: OK, we'll take them when we leave.

Amma (holding out a bag): Your iPod and headphones are in here. Luna sent them. You don't like her visiting, so she didn't come. But she said you'd like to listen to music.

Me (taking the bag): Yes, music might make me feel better. Tell Luna Apa to come.

Amma: I will.

Heera maama (to Amma after several minutes of silence): Let's go then, Apa.

Amma: Let's go. Sunny ma, I brought you some gourd and pumpkin with rice, eat.

With great effort I hold back my tears and say bye to them. I don't walk them to the main door, Heera maama doesn't let me.

Ivan goes off to the kitchen to get himself a cup of tea. I offer to make some for him. He agrees, saying, 'All right, two sugars and one milk please. I'll be in the courtyard.' I go to the kitchen after depositing the food and iPod in my room. I make tea in two disposable cups and take them out to the courtyard. We sit down side by side. 'What did you think of my mother?' I ask.

Ivan: She's a good person.

Me: What did you think of my uncle?

Ivan: He's a good person too.

Me: What do you think of me?

Ivan: You're a good person.

Me: What? A good person, that's all?

Ivan: Ha ha no, I'm kidding.

He puts an arm around me. I move even closer to him. I kiss his cheek. He smiles. I kiss him on his lips. He moves away.

Ivan: No, not on the lips, not here.

Me: Why, aren't you my boyfriend? Am I not your girlfriend?

Ivan: Maybe. But we're in an artificial environment. It's difficult to judge what's true and what's false, what's right and what's wrong—even about our feelings. Let's get out first, then we'll see.

Me: When will we go to home?

Ivan: Go to home? Ha ha.

Me: Ha ha, I realized 'to' is wrong but it slipped out anyway. But you did judge between right and wrong here and laughed.

Ivan: Ha ha. Perhaps you'll understand later where I'm coming from.

Me: OK. Do you know what happened today?

'What happened?' someone asks. Turning to the right, I find Jed, Chris and Belinda sitting on the next bench.

Me: Oh no, how long have you guys been here?

Belinda: Darling, what were you doing that you shouldn't have been?

All of us laugh.

Jed: I saw you looking miserable a little while ago, Sanya, you were crying on your way to your room. What's the matter? All OK now?

Me: No, it's not OK. But I don't want to think about it.

Belinda: About what?

Me: They've forced two new medicines on me. Apparently, I follow boys around, and my mood isn't stable. I think it's because I screamed and cried the other day when they were giving me an injection. Even today I disagreed with the doctor and cried.

Jed: What nonsense! What do you think we can do about it?

The queue at the medicine-room window after dinner seems longer than usual. Jed, Belinda, Chris, all of them are in queue. All of them, along with many others, asking loudly for medicines they don't usually take. Why? It seems to be another form of protest. Give us medication, make us take it till we die. But will the authorities take this protest seriously? Or are they going to dismiss it as the work of raving lunatics? That's exactly what they're doing, they're paying no attention to the protests of the people in the queue. They're ignoring everyone's demands and resentment. In fact they're explaining, as though no one understands, what harm these medicines can do when taken unnecessarily.

Ivan is not in the queue. Nor is he in his room. After searching for him everywhere, in the dining hall, the prayer room, the pool room, the TV lounge, the courtyard, I go back to his room to find him there. A nurse is calling out the names of his medicines one by one, and he's holding his palm out for each and swallowing them with a sip of water, unmoved, as though nothing matters to him.

I go into his room after the nurse leaves. When I ask him how he is, he says his legs are aching terribly, can I massage them? A song in Hindi plays in my head as I massage his legs:

Ek Radha ek Meera
Dono ne Shyam ko chaha
Antar kya dono ki chaah mein bolo
Ek prem deewani, ek daras deewani

There was Radha and there was Meera
Now both of them wanted Shyam
And how did their desires differ?
One sought love and the other, a glimpse

I don't know why this particular song occurs to me, but there must be a reason. I see Ivan smiling gently; his eyes are closed as though he can hear the song playing in my head.

10

The courtyard is visible through Ivan's window. Itchy and several other pigeons are wandering around even at this hour of the night. Their green shoulders and necks are gleaming in the moonlight. Making a great effort, Itchy flutters his wings to fly up to the tall flower pot near Ivan's window. Daisies have bloomed in it around a plant whose name I do not know.

I turn to look at Ivan. In his hurry, he's put his jeans on inside-out. He's lying on his stomach, fast asleep. My eyes fall on the label on his jeans. Going up closer, I find it says, 'Made in Bangladesh'. I am astonished. Did he know everything all along, that something would develop between us? I take a quick glance at my own clothes, they're not in disarray. Why should they be? Ivan had only held me from the back for a moment. I leave his room quietly, taking with me the joy of that moment.

I am able to reach my room more or less without obstacles. Only Philomena stops me on the way, putting her arms around me and saying, 'Hi darling, how're you doing?'

Me: I'm good, and you?

Philomena: Me too. I just needed a hug. Thank you. What's your name again?

Me: My name's Sanya. But what's this, why are you crying?

Philomena: My six-year-old daughter is at home with my mother. She's never lived apart from me. And her grandmother is old, but I'm stuck in the hospital. I just have to go home.

Me: Don't be upset, I'm sure something will be arranged. Have you informed the doctors?

Philomena: I have.

Me: What did they say?

Philomena: They said they would arrange for me to be sent home soon.

Me: You'll be all right then, nothing to worry about.

Philomena: Yes. Thank you, Sanya.

Me: You're welcome. What's that book in your hand?

Philomena: This? It's the Bible.

Me: I see.

Philomena: I'm a Jehovah's Witness.

Me: Jehovah's Witness?

Philomena: Yes, the followers of a particular branch of Christianity are called Jehovah's Witnesses.

Me: I see.

Philomena: Do you want to read my Bible?

Me: Some other time, not today.

Saying bye to Philomena, I go into my room, where I sit on the bed, smiling to myself, overwhelmed by a secret joy over what had happened a short while ago. But the rapture does not last very long, for some people pass my room, laughing, running, knocking their sticks on the floor. Opening the door, I find a group of strangers disappearing in the direction of the rooms on the right, at the other end of the corridor. One of them is using a crutch as he runs, limping. One of his legs is bandaged up to the knee.

I go out of my room, walking in their direction. Who are they? Where have they come from at this hour of the night? Turning to the right at the bend in the corridor, I find it deserted, no one to be seen anywhere. How did the commotion and the laughter disappear in a flash?

I walk down this length of the corridor, turn to the right at the end, then to the right again to return to my room. Suddenly several people overtake me, walking just in front or farther ahead. I look behind me to find several people there as well. The empty corridor is suddenly filled with people.

I stroll along. Some of the faces around me are familiar, some not. I'm looking for Ivan amid the crowd, but I can't see him anywhere. He's probably asleep still. Let him sleep. I am reminded of his sleeping figure.

Suddenly someone says, 'Don't think of him so much, you'll have to pay for it later.'

I look to my left to find Chris walking alongside me.

Me: How did you know what I was thinking? I didn't tell you.

Chris: You don't have to say anything, it's written all over your face.

Me (whispering): But how?

Chris: How? Have you heard of Paul Eckman? The one whose work on facial expressions and emotions . . .

Me (cutting Chris off): How did you hear this question, for that matter? I barely whispered.

Chris: Oh, I have excellent hearing.

I feel Chris is hiding something. I walk slightly faster, to a clearing in the corridor. A little beyond my room there's a pattern on the floor, it makes me think bats have been painted on it at equal distances. And at once Michael, who's been walking in front of me, sits down on the pattern, spreads his arms wide and pretends to fly. It's so strange, how does he know what I'm thinking?

I walk even farther, leaving Michael behind. Looking to my right, I find the glass doors leading to the courtyard. They're rattling loudly, there's a fierce storm blowing outside. For some reason I'm reminded of Count Dracula, as though he has turned into a bat and is flying towards me through the storm. I realize I'm being sucked into the trap of an imposed language. At this moment, I need someone who is in possession of both common sense and compassion. Someone who can talk me out of this whirlpool. Just as Luna Apa had done when I was so scared of the colour brown. If I tell the nurses, they'll only give me medication, which achieves nothing besides making me sick. I'm not taking that route. If I'd been in the habit of watching TV, I could have spent some time in the TV lounge. But who knows whether the people there would have behaved just as weirdly? I'd better go to my room and lie down for some time.

It starts raining heavily as soon as I wrap myself in my blanket. I feel Allah is showering his benediction, that the vampires will no longer be able to come anywhere near me. As the rain intensifies, all my worries about ghouls melt away. There must be some explanation for the strange behaviour I just witnessed, but I don't want to speculate right now. My attention is being drawn to a different incident instead.

It was raining just as torrentially that day. I was completely alone in Abba and Amma's huge house in Carrum Downs. No, I'm not complaining, I loved being alone, loved it very much. My head was always crowded with ideas, and the idea of being by myself was to write those down. So it was to fulfil that wish that Abraham, my ex, had dropped me to my parents', far away from where he and I lived. Abba and Amma were in Bangladesh, which meant the house was empty. I can't describe how good it felt just to breathe in that empty house.

I arranged my material at one end of the enormous dining table. Switching on my laptop, I put on a music DVD, feeling even more inspired to study. Then, suddenly, it seemed to me someone was sitting in Amma's rocking chair, staring at me. I jumped to my feet to get rid of the impression, went to the bathroom and then to the kitchen to drink a glass of water, but the notion persisted.

I went back from the kitchen to the lounge, my head bowed under the weight of a darkness around me that I was entirely unused to.

As soon as I entered the lounge and raised my head, a coil of black smoke leapt at me from the rocking chair. I screamed in terror without even realizing it. I went and sat in the bathroom for a long time to get the smoke off my body. Then, unsure whether I was truly rid of it, I returned to the dinner table in the lounge and tried to concentrate on my work in front of my computer. I could not. My eyes were constantly drawn to the video cassettes of the Bengali TV series *There's No One Anywhere* piled high on the table. Someone seemed to be telling me that there was no one here to protect me. Unable to understand what was going on, I sat down on the sofa and suddenly noticed the DVD cover of the movie *Enemy at the Gates*. At that moment, the sound of a motorcycle convinced me that there was indeed someone outside the house who was going to harm me.

An enemy at the door, and no one to save me. I remained curled up on the sofa. And that was when it began to rain torrentially. That day too, in that situation, I had felt that Allah was showering his blessings, that I would come to no harm. The thunder sounded like Mikail shouting angrily at Shaitan. How wonderful the rain felt that day, it seemed to be protecting me, just like the rain today.

But my situation that day was not like it is now. Back then, I had assumed my sensations were real, but today I know they're being inflicted on me, I can get out of them. All I need is proper help, based on conversation, not medication. The sound of the rain is mingling with my breath, I can tell that I'm falling asleep.

It's quite late when I wake up. The breakfast hour has long passed, but that's not a problem. There's bound to be some food in the kitchen, inshallah. I brush my teeth and go to the kitchen, where I find various fruits, bread, butter, different kinds of jam, breakfast cereal and arrangements for tea laid out on the bench-top, while the fridge contains milk, juice and flavoured yoghurt. Putting together a tray, I head towards Ivan's room. He never eats breakfast, today he can have breakfast in bed.

Ivan's not in his room. Maybe he's gone for a smoke and will be back at any moment. Drawing open the window curtains, I look out but don't see him anywhere in the courtyard, though I do see Nurse Brenda measuring Maria's blood pressure.

I move away from the window; there will be a furore if I'm spotted in Ivan's room. I take the tray back to the dining hall, I can always put a fresh one together when I see him. Sounds of cheerful conversation and laughter draw closer as I begin to eat. Soon a group of women and men enters the dining hall, laughing and talking loudly. The centre of attraction is the withered man with the crutch from last night, dressed in a blue gown. I notice that not only is one of his legs bandaged up to the knee, but his arm is in a sling too. How old can he be? Around 50? He's tall, built like an athlete. He seems very friendly, I can hear frequent bursts of laughter from his group, probably sparked by him.

Despite having one arm in a sling, he holds the door to the courtyard open for the others. Once they've all gone outside, he contrives to follow them. I see he's holding a packet of marsh-mallows in his other hand. On a whim, he turns back halfway, opens the door slightly, pokes his head in and addresses me, 'Want a marshmallow, sweetheart?' I stop eating to smile at him and say, 'No thanks, but thanks for offering.' He returns my smile, closes the door and joins the others outside.

Finishing my meal, I put the tray back in the kitchen and then go looking for Ivan in all the places he might be. He's nowhere to be found. I go back to my room, wondering what to do. That's when I remember the iPod. That's right, I can always listen to music. Taking the iPod out of the drawer, I plug in the headphones and switch it on. After a few songs, Jagjit Singh's 'Ahista Ahista' about Laila and Majnu begins to play. I really love this song, the melody, the rhythm, the entire composition moves me. I feel I'll enjoy it more out in the courtyard.

I go out and sit on a bench in the corner and listen to the song on a loop. There's one part I feel particularly drawn to, so I keep rewinding it:

Jawaan hone lagi jab woh, toh humse kar lia parda
Haya yaklakht aai aur shabab, ahista ahista
When she became a woman, she hid behind the veil
Modesty and youth blossomed together, slowly, slowly

When everyone begins to leave, I realize they've been sitting here all this time. The man with the crutch smiles at me as he goes in. I smile back. All of them disappear inside. The lunch trolleys are here. I'm alone in the courtyard. I'm really enjoying the music, and since I had a late breakfast, I'll go in to eat later.

Most of them have finished eating by the time I go in, they're having dessert. I sit down with a salad sandwich and an ice cream. As I eat, I can hear the man with the crutch say loudly, 'The dessert with rhubarb is so good, my god.' The others join him in praising the dessert with rhubarb. It seems to me they're throwing the word rhubarb at me because I've been listening so many times to the bit in the Jagjit Singh ghazal that has 'shabab' in it. But how do they know what I've been listening to?

On my way to Reception after lunch, I find Ivan outside Philomena's room. He's outside the open door and she's inside. They're talking to each other with smiles, waving their arms. Let them. They're only talking, nothing more.

But is there anything more? I ask Ivan when he goes into his room.

Ivan: What do you mean?

Me: Do you like Philomena?

Ivan: As a friend.

Me: Does she like you?

Ivan: Maybe.

Me: Maybe meaning?

Ivan: Meaning I don't know.

Me: She's very pretty.

Ivan: That's true, she is.

Me: How long have you known her?

Ivan: As long as I've been here.

Me: You knew her before you knew me?

Ivan: Yes.

Me: You liked her from before?

Ivan: As a friend.

Me: OK, never mind. But what are these jeans you're wearing?

Ivan: Oh, I bought them today.

Me: Where were you all morning?

Ivan: They took me shopping.

Me: Show me the label of your jeans.

The label says 'Made in China'. Suddenly I feel I'm no longer so special for him. Ivan leaves the room, I follow him, thinking to myself, 'How peculiar he looks.' He looks back at me briefly. Has he heard my thought? I don't know.

As I open the door to go out into the courtyard, the man with the crutch comes in with his group, he looks at Ivan and asks, 'Did you like the marshmallow?' Ivan says, 'Naah, too soft.'

I feel he's talking about me. I don't like it.

Sitting down on a bench, Ivan takes a cigarette out of a fresh packet and lights it. Then he asks me, 'Can you spare 50 dollars?' Saying, 'I can,' I go to my room, fetch 50 dollars from my purse and give it to him. He seems pleased. We sit in silence for some time before saying goodbye and going off to our respective rooms.

I don't see Ivan in the dining hall that night. I go to his room afterwards, but he's not there either. Only the notebook I gave him, along with another document, are lying on the bed. I open the notebook to find it full of mathematics problems, solved using various laws of physics. My heart swells with pride. I pick the document up for a look—it's a medical report, with Ivan's name, address and phone number written on it. Has he left it here for me, so that I can note down his address and phone number? I'll do that later, let me find out where he is now.

But with Ivan nowhere to be found, I go to sleep. Several hours have passed by the time I wake up. The lunch trolleys are trundling past in the corridor, returning with empty trays. Which means, it's past lunchtime. How odd, how could I have slept for such a long time? After the trolleys have all passed my door, I realize Ivan is standing nearby, talking to a doctor. I think the doctor is saying, 'We don't think you have any problem.' I can't hear any more, but later Ivan tells me they're letting him go today.

I feel bad, but I feel happier that Ivan is going to be released. 'Do you want an ice cream?' he asks. 'No thanks,' I say. Then he asks loudly, appearing a little angry, 'Do you want an ice cream?' I say, 'OK.'

Some of us sit around eating the ice creams that Ivan has bought us, after which I go for a shower. When I come out, Ivan isn't there. He's gone. Totally, utterly, gone! I'm heartbroken, I didn't imagine he'd leave this way, so very soon and so suddenly!

I see Philomena sitting in the courtyard. Did Ivan meet her before leaving? I don't ask her. She seems to be hiding her tears. Why is Philomena crying? Is it for her daughter? I sit down close to her. 'Ek Radha Ek Meera' begins to play in my head again.

Ek rani, ek daasi
Dono Hari prem ke pyaasi
Antar kya dono ke tripti me bolo
Ek jeet na maani,
Ek haar na mani.

One a queen, one a handmaid
Both thirsting for his love
How did their joys differ?
One rejected her conquest
One rejected her loss.

11

Philomena tucks a note into my hand and pulls me into a tight hug. 'Read this only after I'm gone,' she says.

Me: OK. What secret have you put in it?

Philomena: Nothing like that. Still, when you read it, you'll feel I'm near you. You'll like that, and I'll feel good to know you like it.

Me: Really? You'll feel good because I will?

Philomena: Really.

Me: Have you always been so generous?

Philomena: It's all thanks to Jehovah.

Me: I have to get closer to Allah too. I have no note for you, Philomena, but I have lots of love and prayers from the bottom of my heart. I pray that you live happily . . . happily and in love with your daughter. I pray you find someone very special in your life.

Philomena smiles. I hold her tight. She holds me too. Then, with a suitcase in one hand and some bags in the other, she walks out through the doors of the psychiatric ward.

I turn around and start walking to my room so that I can read the note in private. After a few steps, I see the man with the crutch approaching me, although he's no longer using his crutch, he's on a wheelchair. Someone's pushing him, quite swiftly. He seems to suppress a sigh as he passes me, lightly holding a hand out. I touch it without much thought. He continues to hold it out, without withdrawing it. I tremble. What's this, it hasn't even been a week since Ivan left, what's going on here? Am I not in love with Ivan after all? I am. I don't love this man, but there's something in his touch. Which is what? Is it love? Yes, perhaps it *is* a kind of love. There's deep compassion too.

Going into my room, I shut the door and sit in my chair. I notice my hands are shaking as I unfold the note, and that the scene of the man touching my hand with his eyes closed is playing out in front of my eyes. I glance at the note. It says:

> My dearest brave, kind and sweet Sanya,
>
> I'm leaving the psychiatric ward today. Your presence during part of my stay here made it better for me. Last night, when we spent a lot of time together walking up and down the corridor, when I told you about my fears that the air conditioning might be making us sick, and tried to get to know Jehovah a little more, I felt I would remember all of this. You must consult a doctor about your physical weakness and your illness. Tell the authorities of the psychiatric ward about these things. I'm longing to see my daughter, you too must be yearning to go to your loved ones, to be with them. May god fulfil your wishes. My heart says you'll be home soon. Stay well till then.
>
> Lots of love.
>
> Yours,
> Philomena.

I refold the note and put it in the drawer of the bedside table. Then I open my diary. Should I write to Philomena? No, let me write something else. I'm consumed by uncertainty and restlessness about something, maybe writing about it will help make things clear.

Assume you live in a world where no one can be held responsible for anything, for their present actions are directly connected with a process that has been in place for ages, where there is a distinct reason for everything that takes place. In other words, you are caught in a vicious circle of wrongdoing which runs on the written or unwritten laws of the social system. Now, what will you do if you discover yourself imprisoned in such a 'different' social system?

At the outset, you might question the primary medium—language—through which the written and unwritten laws of a society are determined and enforced. You can ask whether the members of this society and you speak the same language. What does 'same language' mean? Is it the external structure of the language—such as Bangla, English, Urdu, etc.? Or is it an internal form that conveys meaning to the smaller societies that exist within the larger? Let us assume that, in most cases, this internal language follows the same rules as the external one, so that you can use some of the characteristics of the external language to capture the internal.

One might assume that everything will become easier if you and the members of this 'different' society use the same language. But this is not always true. Those who speak the same language often introduce complexities and nuances into their discussions by the very virtue of using the same language, which speakers of different languages cannot. When they use different languages, speakers emphasize on simplification and approximations which can be understood by one another. Their conversations make use of signs too. But even though such conversations often begin in simple, easy ways, the limitations of self-expression can make them complicated and obscure and frequently lead to misunderstandings.

Two kinds of complexity are seen here. One of them inspires discussions on subjects with nuance and depth, a path that may look superficially difficult but in fact leads to freedom. The other shows the way to a simplification of the theme, which prevents one from going deep into the subject and discovering it, and oneself, afresh. So this route, despite appearing easy at first glance, is in fact a road to imprisonment.

Does this state of imprisonment manifest itself because of the differences between two languages, or could it be concealed in one particular language—a language whose words are stuck in the form of images in a universal space and time? I've just mentioned being stuck in a particular time, but we know time is not an object—it has no length, breadth or height, dimensions within which something can be trapped. And yet we use object-like symbols to enable ourselves to conceive of even intangible worlds. Many intangible ideas are born through language. Holidaying in Sweden next year, for example. The interval between two points in time, which creates a period, is what we describe as a length of time. Although length and interval are not identical, in certain situations the two can be the same. Similarly, a situation may refer to a place but also to context, and place refers to space but can also indicate context. We will be released from the imprisonment of language only when we stop yoking exact meanings to words.

But one way of looking at it is that the strings of the kites of language are tied to objects. For, language begins with objects. How does a child learn to use language? First, they master the subjects that they can grasp with their senses, the objects and the relationships between them. From this point onwards, their vocabulary develops like the branches of a tree. The nature of their words becomes complex, as does the relationship between word and meaning. The words are no longer grounded, they begin to float in the air. But even now there are remnants of proto language, such as the use of special sounds, in conversations. Often, we accompany our words with gestures and specific facial expressions to convey our thoughts. Before they learn words, babies use this proto language for their conversations, which is quite natural and helpful up to a point. But if a language, after it has spread its branches far and wide, ties down these branches with gestures, daily acts and specific usage of words, or if it determines at the very beginning where the branches will end, then even the infinite becomes restricted. As a result, this language loses its life and is converted into an inanimate corpse.

There is a knock on the door when I get to this stage of my diary entry. I feel somewhat relieved, because although there's a lot more to be written, this seems to be a good place to stop. 'Come in,' I say. Nurse Gary opens the door a crack, pokes his head in and says with a wink, 'As I thought. You've been sent to the naughty corner, haven't you?' I laugh and ask, 'Why, what have I done now?' Gary says, 'Why are you sitting here if you haven't done anything?' I answer in surprise, 'Oh my god, is it dinner time already? I had no idea. Let's go, I'm starving.'

Gary smiles. I shut the door behind me, and start walking towards the dining hall which lies beyond the door to the small courtyard, the prayer room and the pool room. I stop in surprise when I get to the pool room. A young man I don't know is touching up the old painting that covers all of one wall, even modifying it in places. Several pretty girls are gathered around the pool table, watching him, spellbound. I, too, gaze at the room for some time, enchanted. The guy smiles at me and says 'hi'. I flash a smile at him too with a 'hi' and then quickly go into the dining hall.

As soon as I pick up my dinner tray, the man with the crutch beckons to me. 'Sit with us tonight, Sanya.'

Me (taking a seat two chairs away, on his left): There's never a chair free next to you. You're so popular.

Him: Are you jealous of my success or because you can't have me?

Me: What do you mean? Why should I be jealous?

Him: I mean, are you jealous of the people around me who can sit near me while you can't? Or are you jealous of me because I'm popular and you're not?

I stare at him blankly for some time, trying to understand what he's saying and why. He bursts out laughing at my bewilderment, the people around him laugh too. He says, 'No need to take it so seriously, I'm just kidding. I know very well you have no reason to be jealous of anyone, and that you're very popular yourself.'

Me: Popular? Me?

Him: Yes, or how'd I know your name?

Me: That's true, how *do* you?

Him: That's what I'm saying, your name's everywhere.

Me (laughing): But I don't know yours.

Him (laughing): How would you know? I'm not popular. Your servant's name is Steve.

Me: Honoured to know your name, Steve. Come, let's have dinner now.

Steve: Oh yes, you must eat, I'm done. The best part comes now, dessert. Rhubarb. Which one have they put in your tray, have they put the rhubarb?

Me: No, I've got bread-and-butter pudding.

Steve: Oh. The rhubarb dessert is delicious.

The line with shabab from Jagjit Singh's ghazal plays in my head again. I finish my dinner and dessert quietly. When Steve sees I'm about to leave, he stops his conversation with the others and says, 'Taste the rhubarb dessert before you go, you'll miss something if you don't.'

'I'm stuffed, some other day, maybe.'

I pause at the door to the pool room on my way back to see the young man still painting away. But he's alone in there now. He says warmly when he sees me, 'Come in, come inside.'

'No need, I can see from where I am.'

'Come inside, you can't see properly from there. The angle isn't right, the light's shining on the colours, you can't see them clearly.'

I go in and stand with my hands on the pool table. The guy gets up off the floor, wipes his hands on his trousers, shakes my hand and says, 'I'm Paul, and you?' 'I'm Sanya.'

He stands very close to me as I tell him my name. My guilt about feeling good about this makes me turn by back to Paul and put my hands on the table again. Paul stands behind me and reaches for the table with his arms on either side of mine. Sensing the warmth of his body, I duck beneath his right arm and leave.

Back in my room, I gasp for breath. I can't afford to be caught in these webs of love, my life is supposed to be different. Opening my diary, I read today's entry. How about putting this in my hospital file? Nurse Jane photocopies the pages and files them away when I make the suggestion at Reception.

Walking in the corridor after taking my night medication, I see two young men going from Reception towards the ward doors. One of them is spinning a rolled-up piece of paper on his hands. Taking a closer look at it, I discover it's the photocopy of my diary entry. How strange, what do they want with it? Are they by any chance going to rescue me from this system? The questions swirl in my head even after I'm in bed. Eventually I fall asleep.

After breakfast the next morning, Nurse Gloria says she'll check my blood pressure and heart rate, etc. I should go wait in the TV lounge. I watch TV reluctantly as I wait for her. Maria, sitting next to me, keeps flipping channels. She stops at Channel 7, where *The Morning Show* on Saturday is on. In utter astonishment I find a reporter saying exactly the same things that I'd written in my diary, attributing them to someone else.

Nurse Gloria arrives and asks me a few questions before checking my blood pressure, taking down my answers of 'yes', 'no' or ratings. Like every time, some of the questions have to do with whether I see hidden codes in the newspaper or on TV or anywhere else around me. Whether people are talking about me or my activities. As always, I answer 'no'. Since my blood pressure and heart rate are in the normal range, I am free to go.

When I step into the corridor, I find Chris walking in through the ward doors on my right with a large backpack on his shoulders. When he comes closer, I say, 'Hi Chris, where did you go?'

Chris: I went shopping.

Me: You're allowed outside the ward? You went alone?

Chris: Yes, I went alone, I'm allowed to go out, I'm allowed leave. I got overnight leave yesterday. I spent the night at my parents and did some shopping before returning.

Me: Will they give me leave too if I ask?

Chris: Maybe not overnight leave immediately. Maybe they'll start by allowing you into the hospital grounds outside the ward with a staff member. Then they'll let you go out of the hospital for a few hours with your family. Then, finally, overnight leave.

Me: What are the conditions for getting leave?

Chris: You have to follow the instructions of the doctors, nurses and staff in hospital.

Me: OK, got it.

Chris: Oh, guess what, I met Ivan at the shopping centre.

Me: Wow, really? How's he doing?

Chris: Very good.

Me: Did he ask about me?

Chris: No. I don't know why you like Ivan so much, he's a thief.

Me: Of course not. What's he stolen?

Chris: He borrowed my headphones and CD player and didn't bother to return them. He's made off with them.

Me: What are you saying? Can you imagine the number things going through someone's mind when they're leaving? He must have forgotten to return your things. I'm sure you'll get them back once you're out of the hospital.

Chris: Let's hope so. I reminded him again today.

Me: In that case, don't worry.

Chris: I do worry, because he's a thief. Anyway, you won't get it. I'm going to my room, bye.

Me: OK, bye.

I head to the kitchen for some tea. I'm feeling a little upset because Ivan hasn't asked about me. But then that's what he's like, he doesn't say anything, keeps all his thoughts to himself.

Or is that not the case, has he forgotten me? Wondering about these things, I'm almost at the kitchen when I spot Russell the bodybuilder. Suddenly he roars at someone in the dining hall, 'What's that you said? Try saying it again?'

A voice emerges from the dining hall, 'You can't fuckin' just boss me around, I'm a human being and you have to treat me accordingly.'

'Do you know who you're talking to?'

His bellow reverberates through the corridor as the burly Russell runs up to the diminutive Scott and grabs his collar. He shouts abuses, shakes Scott, threatens to punch him.

I begin to cry noisily with rage at this, shouting, 'Russell, you're bullying Scott, let go of him at once.'

Scott begins to cry too and wets his pants. 'Go inside, Sanya,' Russell screams, 'I'm telling you to go inside.'

I go into the kitchen, crying, and read out a sign tacked up on the wall at the top of my voice, 'Violence against staff or patients will not be tolerated in this ward.'

A couple of male staff members prise Russell away. Scott remains sitting on his chair, crying, his head lowered on the dining table. Some of the nurses and staff members go up to him. Nurse Jane sends me to my room. I sit there quietly for an hour or so, and then, when I feel calmer, I return to the kitchen to make tea.

I don't see Scott anywhere. Maybe he's gone off to his room, I don't know. Suddenly I feel a warmth behind me; looking over my shoulder, I find Paul standing there. I tell him, 'Be careful of me, I'm not allowed to follow boys.' Paul responds, 'You're not following me, I'm following you. If anyone's breaking the rules, it's me.' I try to laugh, but end up crying. Paul holds me tightly.

After a shower, I go to the courtyard in the late afternoon. I'm wearing a long sleeveless dress and a scarf. Steve is sitting there too, with several others. He waves me over when he sees me, and makes me sit next to him on his left where there's some space. He looks at me strangely, I find his gaze rather sleazy. He keeps touching my upper arm beneath the scarf, I don't like it at all. I get up and walk to an empty bench in the distance, thinking: this doesn't suit Steve at all. From what I've seen of him, behaving this way is completely out of character for him. Then why is he acting this way? Is it to teach me a lesson? Possibly. I feel he's merely pretending to be sleazy, so that I don't get intimate with boys too easily.

Soon everyone gets up and goes inside, but I keep sitting. Paul shows up and sits down on the bench at the right-hand corner of mine. 'My painting is nearly done,' he says.

Me: Great!

Paul: There's a bit of work left, but someone else will finish it.

Me: Why someone else? Why not you?

Paul: I'm leaving tonight.

Me: OK. Everyone leaves. So will I, someday.

Paul: Yes, you'll be leaving soon too.

He looks at me sadly but lovingly. I feel I owe him a hug. But had I not promised myself a moment ago not to get intimate with boys any more? Still, is a hug really intimate? I get up and give Paul a hug. He holds me tight. I cup his face in my hands and lift it to find his eyes brimming with tears. 'I haven't given you anything,' I tell him, 'but remember me.'

12

Nurse Sylvia is taking me to the cafe. I've got leave for the first time after spending two months in hospital. Accompanied leave of one hour, on the hospital grounds. A long corridor leads from the psychiatric ward to the cafe. At its head stands an automatic double door, which opens with a whine when we go up to it. I taste freedom as soon as I walk through it. I don't think I've ever noticed how beautiful it is on either side of this corridor. Its walls are of glass, beyond which lie a glorious profusion of greenery and trees. I drink it all in thirstily as I walk.

In the cafe, Sylvia asks me what I'd like. So many things are available that I can't make up my mind. Eventually I pick a bottle of blue Gatorade. As I'm about to take the money out of my purse, Sylvia holds out a 50-dollar note and some loose change to the person at the cash counter, just as my PhD supervisor had done when they'd taken me for coffee to the university cafe after I failed my confirmation seminar. To my surprise, I discover the person at the cash counter accepting the coins in the same way from Sylvia, counting them one by one.

How is this possible? Were they there at the university cafe six years ago? I doubt it. Is it just a coincidence then? I don't know. Is it possible that I have thought about the first incident so many times that it has left a strong-enough impression in my mind for others to see or to read? Something like Jacques Benveniste's memory of water?

The theory of the memory of water, applied by the famous scientist Jacques Benveniste, has been used for generations in homoeopathic treatment despite its irrationality in the eyes of science. Homoeopaths believe that the more a medicine is diluted, the more effective it is. Which is why homoeopathic medicines are prepared by repeatedly mixing the medicine with water, and then shaking the mixture using a particular technique. Benveniste had demonstrated that even the most dilute mixture of an anti-serum—in which virtually nothing of the anti-serum is left—affects cells in the same way as the original, pure anti-serum. All his research and commentary suggested that water remembers the properties of anything it comes into contact with, which was why he had termed this special quality 'the memory of water'.

Professor Luc Montagnier (who won the Nobel Prize jointly in 2008 for his work on HIV) got the same results and used the theory of water memory in his HIV research. Montagnier diluted the HIV DNA serially, to the extent where none of the original DNA remained. Then, digitalizing the electromagnetic field of this diluted sample, he sent the sequence file through the internet to a lab far away, where a tube of pure water, which was exposed to the electromagnetic signals reproduced from the digital file, actually 'remembered' it. A sample of this water, which had no physical DNA in it, enabled the DNA to be reconstructed. Although Professor Montagnier termed this process 'transduction', it can effectively be called 'teleportation'.

This transduction or teleportation is possible because water molecules often 'hold hands' to create a circular space which cannot be penetrated from the outside. Electromagnetic signals, however, can enter, and be trapped inside, to form a 'coherent domain'. Even without the physical presence of the DNA in the serially diluted sample, the signals trapped in the coherent domain can be used for transduction and subsequent reconstruction of the DNA.

Our bodies are 70 per cent water and 30 per cent tissue. Has the coherent domain in this 70 per cent of water in my body enabled Sylvia to see the image of the transaction between my PhD supervisor and the cafeteria salesgirl that keeps floating up in front of my eyes?

Because I've been thinking of it repeatedly, coupled with its rich personal significance, the scene is now part of my long-term memory. Does the memory release electromagnetic signals every time I access it during conversations with myself, signals that are then trapped in that circular space between water molecules to create a coherent domain? Can this trapped code be collected from my blood or urine and be used to recreate the scene through transduction? I have no idea. Does anyone know for sure where memories are created, where they are stored? Perhaps all we can say is that repetition is one of the factors that enable the creation of long-term memories, the other being personal significance or meaningfulness. An incident can be meaningful for a number of reasons. It can also be made meaningful in a number of ways—for instance, by finding a connection with, or attaching it to, something significant that already exists in long-term memory. Meaning also lies in a language, such as the way in which a word is used in it. So memories cannot be sought only in the body, they're a matter of language too.

Suddenly I realize Sylvia is walking alongside me. I didn't notice when I left the cafe. Sylvia must have been following me all this while. Now that she's walking by my side, it means it's time to go back. When I apologize for my absentmindedness, she says, 'Don't be silly, It's nothing to worry about.' I go back to the ward. The blue Gatorade, which I haven't yet opened, remains as a memory of the cafe.

Putting the bottle on my desk, I set off for the kitchen, pausing outside the prayer room on the way. Its door is open; old Mrs Anthony is standing inside, reading from a Bible and several patients are sitting around her, on the sofas, and listening. Mrs Anthony stops reading when she sees me and waves me inside. I say I'm going to the kitchen. She points to the chocolate and other snacks she's brought with her. 'You eat them,' I say, 'I'm going to have a cup of tea.'

As I make the tea, I reflect on my conversation with Mrs Anthony last week. I wanted to know more about the Holy Trinity. She didn't say much, perhaps she assumed that I wanted to disgrace her because I belong to a different faith. Perhaps she tried to shame me too in retaliation. Very calmly she asked me, 'Are you a Hindu?'

Me: No, I'm a Muslim.

Mrs Anthony: I see. Do you believe in jihad?

Me: Yes, the Quran does talk about the holy war, but this jihad is only to be used in defence, as it says repeatedly, not for attack. And personally, I believe that the greatest war we wage is against ourselves.

I cannot avoid running into Mrs Anthony again on my way back to my room with my tea. She has come out of the prayer room into the corridor to escort me inside. So I follow.

Daniel, Steve, Andrew and Michelle are sitting on the sofas around her. I take a seat next to Michelle. Mrs Anthony reads two lines aloud from the Bible: 'For the sake of Christ, then, I am content with weakness, insults, hardships, persecutions and calamities. For when I am weak, then I am strong.'

Then she asks us to explain this or to say something on the same lines. At once I raise my hand and say: 'Fa inna ma'al usri yusra / Inna m'al usri yusra.'

When Mrs Anthony looks at me expectantly, I say, 'This is an ayat from the Quran. It means: For, indeed, with hardship there is ease. / Indeed, with hardship there is ease.'

'Yes, that more or less matches the Bible,' says Mrs Anthony. 'Does anyone want to add anything? Go ahead, don't hesitate. What do you think of when you hear this verse from the Bible? A personal struggle of some kind? How will you explain these lines?'

Raising her hand, Michelle says, 'You insulted me last week, but I'm here at the group discussion without taking it to heart. This is proof of my resilience. Your insult has made me stronger.'

'I don't know what you're talking about, Michelle,' says Mrs Anthony. 'I haven't insulted you in any way whatsoever. Anyway, it's time to sing.' She begins to sing a hymn in a mezzo-soprano voice, and Michelle falls asleep almost at once. She begins to snore, and her mouth falls open. Steve gets up and leaves, followed immediately by Daniel and Andrew.

I don't understand why Michelle falls asleep suddenly. Was she very tired? Maybe she didn't sleep last night? But that's not how she looked. And did the others leave because she fell asleep, or was there some other reason?

To find out, I take my cup to the kitchen and then, about to follow the others into the courtyard, pause at the dining hall. Luna Apa, Abba and Amma are here to see me. I'm meeting Luna after ages but I feel a bit embarrassed to go up to her. I've been keeping away from her all this while. When she sees me, Luna holds out her arms and says, 'Santu!'

Her warmth makes me want to cry. I don't say anything, I only pull a chair up to them. 'How are you, baba?' asks Abba.

Me: Very well.

Amma: I've got some bhuna khichuri and tandoori chicken for you. Eat it now.

Dominic comes in just as I'm drawing the boxes towards me.

Dominic: How're you doing, Ahmed?

Abba: I'm very well, and you?

Dominic: I'm good too, thank you.

Abba: Good to know.

Dominic: I have some good news.

Abba: And what's that?

Dominic: Father Moran's coming to take me away.

Abba: Who's Father Moran?

Dominic: Oh, he's the United Church priest.

Abba: I see. Does he know you?

Dominic: Oh yes, he knows me very well.

Me: My mother's cooked something for me, Dominic. Would you like some?

Dominic: Oh, thank you Sanya, you're very kind. I'd be very happy to eat a little if you share it with me. What has your mother brought? (He's about to open the boxes.)

Luna Apa: Hey, don't touch those. You can watch from a distance. Sanya will serve you, you can eat when she does. (Turning towards Amma, she continues in Bangla.) This man was about to put his dirty hands on Santu's food, Amma, but she doesn't say anything.

Amma (turning towards Luna): He didn't touch it though, he didn't understand, baba.

I share my food with Dominic. He says he doesn't want chicken, just some of the yellow rice will do. That's what I serve him, he begins to eat with great relish while I watch him with great satisfaction.

I am on my way back after walking Abba, Amma and Luna Apa to the door when someone calls out my name. I turn to find Dr Nevin standing near Reception with a broad smile. 'Do you have some time to spare?' he asks me. 'I haven't spoken properly with you in a long time, I thought we could catch up.'

Me: I have plenty of time.

Dr Nevin: Will you join me in Interview Room Two then?

Me: Right now?

Dr Nevin: Yes. We can also discuss your ideas on various things if you like.

Me: OK. May I get my diary?

Dr Nevin: Sure.

I fetch my diary and go into Interview Room Two. Only Dr Nevin and a younger girl are in there today. 'You may sit, Sanya,' Dr Nevin says. Pointing to the girl, he says, 'Do you mind if our final-year student Natalie remains in the room during the interview?'

Me: Of course not, why should I?

Dr Nevin: All right then, let's start. You had your first leave today, how does it feel to have gone outside the ward?

Me: Feels great.

Dr Nevin: I'm sure you know you were given leave because we're pleased with your behaviour.

Me: Yes, I know.

Dr Nevin: What changes do you see in yourself now?

Me: I let them give me injections, I don't cry. I take lithium regularly even though I know I don't need it. I even take Olanzapine, which makes me disoriented.

Dr Nevin: They've been prescribed for you because your body needs them.

Me: OK.

Dr Nevin: Look how stable your mood is after regular doses of lithium.

Me: This has nothing to do with lithium, my mood was always stable. I was angry, it seemed wrong to force medication on me, and that was mistaken for mood instability. I'm not angry any more because I have explained to myself that if I refuse the prescribed drugs, I'll be given others instead. Which is why I've decided that I'll continue to take lithium, even though it's poison. Or else I'll be killed even more quickly with other kinds of poison.

Dr Nevin: I can see you're still lacking in insight. You still don't realize there's something wrong with you.

Me: There's nothing particularly wrong with me. And even if there is, medication is not the right way to treat it.

Dr Nevin: What is the right way in your view?

Me: With language. Through conversations.

Dr Nevin: That's possible too. Counselling can be arranged simultaneously with medication.

Me: Not simultaneously, through conversation alone. And it wouldn't be conventional counselling, not the standard questions and answers of cognitive psychology. None of these simplistic and positivist questions and answers like how are you, so-so, what do you like doing, I like drawing, will do. You can't tell anything from them, you only get to know the conscious opinion of the respondent about themselves. There's no way of telling whether they're right or wrong, even if the answers are given honestly.

Dr Nevin: Why not, if the answers are given honestly?

Me: Because honesty and accuracy are not the same thing. The answer might be honest, but the question remains: in what way is the person's identity developing, how much and along what lines?

Dr Nevin: What's to be done in that case?

Me: First, there must be excellent rapport between the patient and the therapist, a relationship of trust. Then, a skilled therapist will examine through close and detailed observation just where the problem lies. Often, locating the source of the problem correctly also yields a situation. I'm telling you all this because at one level I trust you. I wouldn't have said so many things to Dr Wong, because that would have meant being stuffed with medication at once.

Dr Nevin: Ha ha. I've read some of what you wrote that's in your patient file. You're undoubtedly a good writer. But then, as doctors, we have to follow some rules and regulations too. Besides, the treatment you're proposing is neither practical nor economically feasible for so many patients. Moreover, many of the patients prefer medication, and we've seen it works, too.

Me: How do you know it's the medication that works? Were specific controls applied for different patients? Were placebos tried?

Dr Nevin: No, those may not have been necessary, because the medicines had been tested before being put out in the market. Anyway, we were talking about the things you write. Is there anything in your diary that you'd like to read out? I've read samples of your recent writing. You could read out something from the beginning.

I try to read the entries from the first page of the diary and stumble over the words. It's the same with the next two pages, I cannot read them. It seems that the meaning of every sentence has changed between the beginning and the end. But that's not what I say, what I say is, 'Looks like I've been jumping from one idea to the next.'

Dr Nevin: Exactly, your thoughts weren't coherent when you were hospitalized.

Me: And that's influenced my language, perhaps? Now you just helped me see this by interacting with me through language. And I saw it by using my current use of the language to analyse my use of the language then.

Dr Nevin: I'm not denying the role of language. But your condition would not have improved without medication.

Me: But the mind is not the body, it's not an object. Mental issues, mental problems are not sensations that can be fixed with things, with objects, with medicine.

Dr Nevin: What is the mind then?

Me: The mind cannot be defined. Defining it would turn it into an object. What we must examine instead is how the mind manifests itself to us.

Dr Nevin: How does the mind manifest itself?

Me: Through our thoughts, through our senses. These thoughts and senses appear to us in particular contexts. As for us, we're individuals, we're subjects. It is because we're not just bodies, not just objects, that we're changing and developing all the time. And so the same things, the same environment, can affect each of us differently. A therapist, a psychologist, must be sensitive to all of this. Medication cannot be sensitive. Besides, the use of medicines assumes causation in mental life just like in physical life. But mental life is lived in the space of reason, not of causation.

Dr Nevin: Meaning?

Me: Meaning, our thoughts and feelings do not emerge as parcels after specific chemical reactions. So their production cannot be increased or decreased by administering medicines. If that were the case, you would have to consider chemicals to be the cause for generating thoughts and feelings, you would have to imagine these thoughts and feelings are nothing but biological products or objects.

Dr Nevin: Are you trying to say thoughts and feelings have no physical basis?

Me: No, I'm not saying that. If we accept that there is a relationship between the mind and the body, then there is definitely a physical basis to thoughts and feelings. But these thoughts and feelings do not remain unchanged from childhood, they develop as we grow up, they become desomatized.

Dr Nevin: I don't understand. What do you mean desomatized?

Me: I mean they're loosened from the body.

Dr Nevin: How?

Me: When a baby laughs or cries, one can surmise the reason. Most of the time the cause is physical. Maybe the baby is hungry or sleepy or physically satisfied or dissatisfied. When they grow a little older and interact with us through proto language, they can be seen expressing some basic emotions. When they grow even older and master language, their thoughts develop much more, then they can be seen expressing self-conscious emotions, such as pride, shame, guilt, etc. It is through language that thoughts and feelings are developed and expressed. The mental world of a healthy adult is immersed in language. Even when they're alone, they're listening to music or reading, or talking to themselves while cooking, or drawing pictures. Language is the source of their thoughts and feelings. They pour these thoughts and feelings into it, and this is what can create confusion in their mental world. Language alone can unsnarl it, medication cannot.

Dr Nevin: All right, I can see you're passionate about your research. But you have to prove these claims. Have you considered what you'll do after you're released from hospital? Will you go back to your PhD?

Me: I hope to. And even if I cannot prove all of this, I hope to be able to provide convincing arguments. Kabiruddin Chacha, a friend of my father's, said something about proof once.

Dr Nevin: What did he say?

Me: He said, when we talk to each other, the tone we use, the words we choose, the grace with which we express ourselves, all point to something different. A meaning that is not directly contained in what we say. The person being addressed understands what is being hinted at. They don't say anything, for what is hinted at cannot be proven.

Dr Nevin: In the case of science though, evidence-based research is the new trend.

Me: Maybe, but following the trend or not depends a lot on the researcher. Jacque Benveniste, for example, didn't follow the trend, and was considered for a Nobel Prize. He died defending the memory of water.

Dr Nevin: OK. Yeah, I think I've heard of it. It was on TV a long time ago. All right, that's enough for today. Good luck with everything.

Me: Thank you, Dr Nevin.

Dr Nevin: You're most welcome, Sanya.

I leave the interview room and take a couple of rounds in the corridor, by which time the lunch trolleys arrive. I eat lunch quietly and then go into the second TV lounge. There's no one else there, and the TV isn't on either. I'm here just so I can sit by myself for some time somewhere other than in my room. A few minutes later, I find Peter standing at the door.

Peter's come to this ward only a week ago. I know nothing about him, all I know is his name. 'Hi Peter,' I say. He says nothing at first. Then, taking something like a kids' videogame machine out of his pocket, he begins pressing some keys on it and says, 'Hi.'

At once my head tilts to one side. I seem to fall asleep for a moment before waking up immediately afterwards. There's another click. Once again, I fall asleep and then wake up. This sequence is repeated several times. Then Nurse Gary turns up from somewhere and leads Peter away.

I get up. I simply hate losing all control over myself in this way. Is this what they call hypnosis? Perhaps. Did Mrs Anthony hypnotize Michelle? Was that why Steve and the rest of them got up and left?

Leaving the TV lounge, I enter the dining hall on the right. An art-and-crafts session is underway. The dining tables have been gathered together, and two people are seated on either side of each table, drawing and painting. Some are making different patterns by cutting coloured paper. I walk around the tables, looking at their work. The room is quiet but lively—my passivity and weariness are swept away. I go up to Dominic. Who could have told from the dirty clothes he wears or from his conversation how beautifully he draws and paints?

At the insistence of the instructor, I draw up a chair too and sit down with paper and paintbrush. I've never painted without drawing first, I paint a sunset over water. Maybe it's a copy of the orange and blue waves on the concrete wall of the small courtyard adjoining the corrugated tin fence that can be seen from the dining hall. But I paint a number of snakes at the bottom of the water, coming to life as the sun sets.

As I paint, I notice that Dominic has completed his painting and is now cutting paper to make patterns. As soon as our eyes meet, he unfolds it to show me the design—a group of people holding hands. When the art session ends this group of paper people holding hands is pinned to the upper half of the dining hall window.

I sit there for some time, gazing at the new look of the dining hall. When I get up finally, Steve comes up to me to say he's leaving today. He wants to buy his daughter a gift, but he has no money, can I spare 50 dollars?

I am indebted to Steve in a way, I reflect. He has taught me a sort of restraint. And since the gift is for his daughter, I might as well give him my last 50-dollar note.

But I have a sudden suspicion once I give him the money. Why does everyone ask me for 50 cents or 50 dollars? Does the number 50 have some significance? Or the number five?

I go out into the courtyard and sit down next to Dominic. 'When will Father Moran come to take you away?' I ask. Dominic glances at me with a mixture of anger and sadness. I cannot quite recognize him with this look in his eyes. He asks me a counter question, 'Do we deserve to be here, Sanya, do we deserve to be here?'

13

In less than two weeks after the conversation with Dominic, I am released from the hospital.

Nurses from the mental-health centre associated with the hospital visit me at home to give me injections and oral medication for the first six months. Thereafter, I buy the prescribed medicines and take them myself, and despite various physical and mental challenges, visit the health centre for injections.

Three years pass.

A sunny morning. I am standing at the window, the soft sunshine bathing my face. I ask a man who's passing by on the road whether someone in a green longshirt is on the bridge. He can't say for sure. Suddenly a storm begins to rage, and my eyes close under the onslaught of the wind. I open my eyes, here I am, still at the window, but nothing is visible through the light, the mist and the storm.

After some time, I realize I am in fact lying down, facing the wall. The morning sunlight is bouncing off the walls of my room.

I sit up in bed. I am suddenly reminded of the hospital. I notice some resemblances between today's dream and its subsequent reality and the fence of corrugated tin I could see from the dining hall, the reflection of the moving cars in the rainwater gathered in the trench below it, the blue and orange waves painted on the concrete wall.

Magic realism? Can both the scenes be considered magic realism? But today's incident is more real than the hospital fence, rather it's more personal.

Are the corrugated tin wall and the fence painted over with waves still the same? Or has everything changed in the past three years? I recall the sunset I had painted on the basis of these things. And Dominic? His painting? His art was so good, who knows where he is now? No one keeps track of the others after getting out of hospital.

I brush my teeth, get dressed and go downstairs. No one at home is up yet, the sun seems to have risen a little early today. It's only seven in the morning, and even though it's winter, it's already bright out there, even though it's winter.

I pick up the front-door keys. Let me go for a walk before the rest of them wake up.

When I step outside, the frost on the car windshield, which I see but don't touch, makes me realize how cold it is. My body feels quite warm these days. Amma thinks I'm about to get a fever, but that's just an expression of her love, she always feels that way. Still, is Amma a little upset with me these days? Is this what she's trying to convey to me, or at least hint at, when she tells me all the time that I'm sick? Like when I told her the other day that I always feel sleepy, she said, 'Mental patients need extra sleep.'

Luna Apa and Abba have also been behaving peculiarly this past week. Luna Apa keeps asking me annoyingly at regular intervals whether I'm OK. And Abba seems eager to eat from the same plate as me after I have washed it, he'll use the cutlery I used, he'll sit exactly where I was sitting.

All of them are acting strange. As though they're speaking in a different, coded language that I do not understand at all. So I've been trying to avoid them as much as possible. I do my own laundry separately in the washing machine, buy my own food, make noodles for myself. For these tasks might also send them signals in their own language.

The pavement runs just outside the house. Since the pavement on this side is in the shade now, I cross the road to the sunlit one. Two magpies are sitting in single file on top of an electric or telephone pole in the most unusual fashion, warbling in their magnificent voices with their beaks raised towards the sky.

I gaze at them in surprise for some time. I have never seen magpies sitting in a row like this. Even though others shoo them away, I like them. I see them at churches and mosques, although I don't know whether they're given food at these places.

I walk on, my back soaking up the loving touch of the sunlight. Across the road, a little farther ahead, a tree with deep pink flowers is throwing a shadow on the pavement over the high fence of the house on whose grounds it stands. The flowers are so lovely, the tree is a favourite of mine. I cross the road again and step on the pavement nestling in the shade, walking slowly over the pink petals strewn on the ground beneath the flowering tree—as though it's my wedding.

I remember Tanvir. It's 3 or 3.30 in the morning in Bangladesh. It isn't right to call him at this hour. Let the poor fellow sleep, he's under a lot of pressure at work. Besides, I've made his life miserable this past week.

I continue walking in the sunlight, switching pavements every now and then. Passing another pole, suddenly I hear magpies again. I look up to discover, oh my god, two more magpies perched just like the ones I saw earlier, warbling, their beaks held up to the sky. A little later I see the same sight again, and then over and over again as I walk back.

When I'm almost home I see something else that's strange. A small cat of our neighbour's jumps from the fence to the ground, lifts a paw and freezes—just like a statue. As I walk past it apprehensively, it starts moving again.

Why are all these strange things taking place at the same time? Is there some special significance to them? I wait for it to be 2 p.m., so that I can call Tanvir, wake him up and tell him everything.

When I get back home, I eat breakfast and take a cup of tea upstairs. Locking my door, I switch on the computer. I put up a status update about Amma's Facebook post yesterday: 'In her caption to the photo she posted, Amma wrote, "Diltaj Apa's red roses look beautiful amidst fern leaves." I find this caption interesting. Because I wouldn't have used the words "look beautiful"; I'd have written, "Diltaj Apa's red roses amidst fern leaves." '

I think 'look beautiful' is a form of decisive assertiveness here, the expression of a certain self-confidence which does not wait for anyone else's approval. I've noticed Amma doesn't count the number of likes or comments after a status update or a post, which I waste a lot of time on.

It's not as though I'm suggesting that expressing our feelings in a sentence will automatically help us be assertive, or that Amma is always assertive. The reason may be that, first, spoken language does not work in the same way as written language, and second, our, meaning adults', sense of 'self' has already been constructed—not that it cannot be reconstructed, or that it isn't reconstructed every day, but that needs a system to be followed. I have a great deal more to learn about this.

Soon after writing this update I discover a songbird perched on the antenna on the roof next door, chirping continuously. I'm so sleepy my eyes are closing. But I don't want to sleep now, I have so many things to do, yet I can barely sit here, I'm so overcome with sleep. I manage to switch off the computer and lie down, falling asleep instantly.

I wake up at exactly 2 p.m. to the cry of a dove. This has been happening frequently of late, I glance at the watch at very precise times—exactly 10 a.m., or 2 p.m., or 3 p.m., and so on. I call Tanvir at once. He likes being called at precise moments. Answering the call, he says, 'Wake me up later.'

Me: OK.

Tanvir: You're well?

Me: I am, but strange things are happening around me.

Tanvir (shaking the sleep off his voice): Like what?

Me: Never mind, I'll tell you later. Sleep now, baba.

Tanvir: I'm not sleepy any more. Tell me now.

I tell him about the magpies and the frozen cat in detail.

Tanvir: Oh, is that what happened? I must say it's very interesting. Birds are very strange, their world is strange too. We are yet to know a great deal about them and their world. There's no need to compare any of this to yourself. Maybe something's happening in their world today, which is why you saw them doing the things they were doing. And as for the cat incident, cats do this, dogs too. I've seen it too. Many times.

Me: OK.

Tanvir: Better now?

Me: Better.

Tanvir: Is anything else giving you trouble?

Me: It is, but that's ongoing.

Tanvir: No problem, tell me.

Me: I'd better not, what if it makes you angry?

Tanvir: Go ahead, don't worry.

Me: Remember I told you about the strange way Abba, Amma and Luna Apa are behaving? It hasn't stopped.

Tanvir: They love you very much, baba. Your mother's worried about you. She loves you a lot, that's where her worry's coming from. Didn't you tell me how hard she worked every day during your depression? Your father sees himself in you, he holds a special love and respect for you. And Luna Apa can't stand me, I often find her annoying too, but she can give up her life for you. Don't forget she quit her great job in New Zealand and came back just for you. How many brothers or sisters in the world would do that?

Me: All right, I get it. But why are they doing all this?

Tanvir: Oh, they're not doing anything, they're not doing anything at all, you're just imagining things. No one's speaking in a secret language. You're always accusing people of doing things, why are you so negative about everything? So long as you do the right things yourself everything will be fine.

Me: Why're you getting angry?

Tanvir: How many times can I say the same thing?

Me (crying): OK, bye.

Tanvir: Oh, don't cry, baba, I can't take it when you cry. I'm sorry, I shouldn't have been angry. Forgive me. I feel helpless when you start crying.

Me: And what about me? No one believes me, everyone thinks I'm crazy. You're the only one I open my heart to, but you don't believe me either.

Tanvir: Assume I believe you, baba, will that solve the problem? Everyone calls you crazy, now they'll call me crazy too. Will that help? Life is full of problems, we have to find the solutions to them, we can't just obsess about them.

Me: You're right. I'm good now. You'd better get ready to go to work.

Tanvir: Are you sure?

Me: I'm sure.

Tanvir: Call me the moment you feel even slightly troubled, no matter how busy I am.

Me: OK.

Tanvir: Love you, baba.

Me: Love you, babu.

After the call, I shower and pray. It makes me calm. I decide to eat whatever Amma has made, to not just survive on noodles.

Luna Apa calls me just as I'm about to go downstairs for lunch to tell me that the CATT people are coming to see me this evening. As always, I say nothing, but it makes me a little worried.

Are all of them going to gang up and send me to hospital again? Then I ask myself: what harm will it do if they do send me? I try to recollect some beautiful memories connected with the hospital. There's Ifa putting up my laundry to dry in the room. My niece Karimunnesa sits next to me, urging me to have some guava. The priest holds my hands, praying for me. Rafiq Sahib and Maama standing near my bed. Rafiq Sahib is reciting Surah Yasin. All of them want me to be well. Perhaps they don't know what they can do to ensure this, but all of them love me. Once I feel calmer, I go out of my room.

The doorbell rings as soon as I go downstairs. I open the door to find Ifa's husband Ashiq and daughter Karimunnesa standing outside, both carrying bags of food. Ifa is helping her two-and-a-half-year-old daughter Rokeya out of the car.

I stand aside to let them in. They take the house over with their warmth and cheer. Rokeya is incredibly loveable, she keeps running up to me, laughing, and throwing herself into my lap. She plays with me, prattles on in her own language. My mood is lifted.

After dinner, Rokeya performs the 'Johnny Johnny Yes Papa' nursery rhyme for us, using the words altered by Ashiq to show off her power of speech. Here's how the exchange goes:

Ashiq: Roku Roku.

Rokeya: Yes, Daddy.

Ashiq: Eating lollies?

Rokeya: No, Daddy.

Ashiq: Telling lies?

Rokeya: No, Daddy.

Ashiq: Open your mouth.

Rokeya: Ha ha ha.

Then Rokeya takes over and plays the game with everyone else, starting the first round with 'daddy daddy' addressed to Ashiq, followed by 'mummy mummy' meant for Ifa. The next round is 'Cori Cori' for Karimunnesa, and then 'Sunny Sunny' for me. All of us play with Rokeya.

Although it's fun for her at first, as the game continues it seems to me that Rokeya's trapped in a loop. She can't get out of it, and no one's helping her. I don't either, because I might be mistaken. I stand up to find Luna Apa coming in through the garage door. As soon as she says 'Roku' and holds her arms out, Rokeya exchanges pleasantries with her in her own language, relieving me of my worry.

Soon the doorbell rings again. Abba opens the door, ushers in two young guys from CATT and leads them into the lounge. I'm a little nervous: what if I say something wrong and they take me to hospital?

In the lounge, I see it's Nick and Gagaan from three years ago. I say 'hi' and sit down on a sofa.

Nick: Hi Sanya, remember us?

Me: I do.

Gagaan: We were here a few years ago to check on you.

Me: Yeah, I remember everything.

Nick: We're here today because your sister Luna says you often forget to take your medication. Do you?

Me: Yeah, I forgot a couple of times, and one day I skipped it deliberately.

Nick: Which medication are we talking about?

Me: Lithium.

Gagaan: We're here to make sure you don't forget to take your medicine regularly.

Nick: What were you thinking when you skipped the lithium deliberately? Don't you trust this medicine?

Me: I don't trust psychiatric medicine in general. Including lithium. And even if it is particularly useful in some cases, I still don't think I need it, because my mood's quite stable. Besides, I have diabetes. My psychiatrist Dr Sanghvi had said lithium interferes with diabetes medication. I took my diabetes medicine very late in the night the day I skipped lithium. Normally, I take the lithium an hour after my diabetes pill. That night I fell asleep as soon as I took my diabetes medication.

Nick: I'm surprised to hear Dr Sanghvi said lithium interferes with diabetes medication. I've never heard anything like this. Can you please get all your medicines here?

I get all my medicines, and show them one by one to Nick, standing near him. At that moment Luna Apa enters, gives me a strong backrub from my shoulders all the way down to my hips, and then sits on the sofa in the corner.

I don't understand why she does this. I don't like it, it feels very intrusive. My scarf is displaced.

I feel some aggression and contempt in the powerful backrub. I remain standing where I am and begin to weep.

Nick asks me why I'm crying. True to my nature, I cannot answer him immediately, I just keep weeping instead. When the question is repeated a little later, I tell myself that they won't see the context of my tears. They won't realize that I've been annoyed with Luna Apa for some time already. Nor will they consider the fact that she's never done anything like this before. Backrubs are nice, they'll say, who cries when given a backrub? I say, 'I'm crying because of the sympathy shown by my sister. Sympathy makes me cry.'

Nick: You're very lucky to have a sister like her.

Me: Yes, my sister buys me lots of clothes, she wants to buy me many things.

Nick: OK, that's great, isn't it?

Me: Yeah, these are demonstrations of love, right?

Nick: Yeah, but you don't sound convinced at all. Don't you think your family loves you?

Me: Maybe they do, but in their own way, they don't love the real me.

Nick: Maybe they don't know the real you.

Me: That's true.

Nick: Hmm. That's enough for today. We have to go to a couple of other places too. Why don't you take your medicines for the night here in front of us?

After I take the medicines Nick and Gagaan say goodbye to everyone and leave, but before going they tell me they'll keep me under surveillance for some time to make sure I take my medicines regularly. They feel I'm a little unwell, but that doesn't necessarily mean I have to go to hospital.

Upstairs, I switch on my computer to see if I can get hold of Tanvir on Facebook Messenger. I do, but not for long. They're taking a tea break at work in his office now, but he has a meeting afterwards, he can only talk to me briefly right now. So that's what we do.

Tanvir: So, babu, how're you doing?

Me: Ifa and her family had come with lots of food. We ate together, then I played with Rokeya, I had a good time. Then the CATT people came.

Tanvir: What did the CATT people say?

Me: They think I'm a little unwell, but I may not have to go to hospital.

Tanvir: What else did they say?

Me: That I'll have to take my medicines in their presence for the next one or two weeks.

Tanvir: OK. You're OK, that apart?

Me: I am, but I cried in front of them.

Tanvir: What did you have to do that for?

Me: Do you think I cried deliberately?

Tanvir: Did anything happen to make you cry?

I tell him everything.

Tanvir: Can I tell you something, babu?

Me: Do.

Tanvir: You're in an oversensitive state. You've been obsessing with insignificant things this past week.

Me: Such as?

Tanvir: You showed me the photo posted by Mono-bhai the other day. Either because of Photoshop or some other reason, your left arm's been cut off or can't be seen. You drew a comparison with something Luna Apa had posted much earlier about your research, where the left collar of Vygotsky's shirt was either cut off or folded.

Me: You don't think it was peculiar?

Tanvir: You didn't consider the possibility it might be pure coincidence, or an accident, or even someone being naughty or making a joke?

Me: Hmm.

Tanvir: You must get out of these things. Else you'll sink again. This is how it starts, I think.

Me: How to get out?

Tanvir: That depends mostly on you, baba. I'll try to help you as much as I can. Now, with your permission, may I go? I'm late already. Don't read or write now, just brush your teeth, pray, and sleep peacefully. Make sure you sleep.

Me: OK.

Tanvir: Allah Hafez.

Me: Allah Hafez.

The following week passes the same way. I write during day time, and take Amma shopping nearby. In the evening, two people from CATT turn up at home to make sure I take my medicines. Most of the time Nick is one of them, which gives me some assurance of fairness despite the injustice of being forced to take the pills.

One day, I drive Abba to his oculist, a long way from home, when I suddenly notice nothing but black and white cars around us. I cannot see any car of a different colour besides ours. And on the back of a truck which has been driving alongside us for a long time it says: Mainfreight. Special people. Special company.

I start interpreting these things and then stop at once. I recall what Tanvir said, I mustn't allow myself to be drowned in these things, I have to get out. Still I tell Tanvir about the black and white cars. He says, 'These are the two most popular colours for cars right now. People have stopped buying other colours. That explains why you saw so many.'

In the evening, the CATT personnel say I'm looking much better, that the illness they'd observed has gone. So they will no longer visit me. But I mustn't miss my medicines, I should make sure someone from the family sees me take them.

I don't like such coercion. Isn't my family also responsible for my having to take medication in the first place, and on top of that, for being asked to take it in their presence? But for now I forget all this, and the joy of not having to go to hospital brings up a song inside my head:

The jasmine whispers to the bee
I know you and you know me

And at that very moment Amma, who's drawing the curtains in the family room, hums:

Your world is a riot of flowers
I cry in the desert
Oh dear lotus
Won't you ever know
How helpless I am

I flash a look at Amma. She looks at me too. I race upstairs to my room.

14

A blue folder lies on the desk. The picture I drew three years ago slips out when I open it. I had begun drawing it after Monet's painting, as Luna Apa had suggested. Later it took a different turn and became a picture of my own:

The willows on the edge of the mainland are weeping. A lotus with a long stalk has bloomed in the pond kept alive by those tears. It wanders around on the surface of the pond.

The water flows around an island created with the soil dug up to make the pond. Some of the trees on this island are connected to one another and have grown intertwined. Only one of the trees stands apart. It's been born on the island, it's an island itself. Flowers have bloomed to signify the love between this tree and the others that have grown collectively.

The island is connected to the mainland by a footbridge, the steps leading down to the edge of the water. The people of the mainland use the bridge to talk to the lotus—so the source of their information is that lotus.

Meanwhile the willows weep. They have something to say. Only the rows of trees indistinguishable from one another have nothing to say, they talk only among themselves, in secret.

The tree cut off from the rest stands with clumps of flowers next to it, as though it's a reflection of the large tree on the mainland in the distance. Flowers are blooming near that tree too. Its top is almost touching the clouds—where the birds fly.